Backlash

Dale Graham

A Black Horse Western

ROBERT HALE

© Dale Graham 2020
First published in Great Britain 2020

ISBN 978-0-7198-3115-7

The Crowood Press
The Stable Block
Crowood Lane
Ramsbury
Marlborough
Wiltshire SN8 2HR

www.bhwesterns.com

Robert Hale is an imprint
of The Crowood Press

Typeset by
Derek Doyle & Associates, Shaw Heath
Printed and bound in Great Britain by
4Bind Ltd, Stevenage, SG1 2XT

AUTHOR'S NOTE

Arguably the three most iconic symbols that epitomize our enduring fascination with the American West are the Colt .45, the Stetson hat and, last but not least, the overland stagecoach. All three, and more, feature in the story that is to follow. But it is with the overland stagecoach, together with the men who drove them, that special mention is felt necessary before we begin.

As the Frontier continued to move inexorably westwards, so the need to keep pace with this relentless expansion grew rapidly. Once the wagon trains had populated outlying territory, the movement of people began in earnest. The earliest need for efficient and regular mail deliveries came from California gold miners. And it was Alexander Todd who in 1849 struck his own form of paydirt by furnishing that need. He charged the miners 5 per cent of the value of their gold, thereby effectively making his fortune.

Other entrepreneurs soon followed Todd's lead. Most notable in the early years was the freighting company of William Russell, along with his partners, Majors and Waddell. They soon included stage-coaches to cater for the increase in personal travel, and for carrying the US mail. In addition to a well organized system of relay stations at regular intervals, their success in this field was also due to the use of the superbly crafted Concord stagecoach.

This was invented by the Abbott Downing Company in 1827, and built in their New Hampshire Concord factory. Over 3,000 were pro-duced before the motor vehicle made them obsolete in 1899. Others tried to emulate the Concord, but none could overshadow these superb vehicles. The coaches could accommodate nine indoor passengers with twelve up top, sitting on luggage. They were brightly coloured in a red and gold livery. Extra comfort was offered in the form of plush seating and ox-hide shock absorbers on which the coach body was suspended. Even so, the cross-country trek was never less than an arduous undertaking.

It was Russell who operated the world-famous pony express service carrying mail between St Joseph and Sacramento. Switching horses every fifteen miles, young riders, including Buffalo Bill Cody, braved all manner of hazards to complete the journey in ten days. The record was an incredible seven days in 1861 to bring President Abraham Lincoln's inaugural address to California. Pay was good, but it was adventure and a sense of bravado that were the main attractions of the job. Unfortunately this audacious enterprise only lasted eighteen months, being superseded by the much faster telegraph of the Western Union.

The ubiquitous stagecoach was a more permanent form of overland transport. John Butterfield established a southerly route stretching from San Francisco to St Louis, Missouri, to avoid the harsh northern winters. Covering almost 3,000 miles, the journey was scheduled for twenty-five days with relay stations every fifty miles, offering basic facilities for passengers. Due to the rocky terrain, he devised a new type of celerity wagon, which was smaller and hauled by mules. This bold endeavour only lasted a mere three years, but established the principle of good time-keeping and reliability. Ticket prices were certainly not cheap. But there was rarely a vacant seat on these overland routes. Assuredly the most enduring of these stagecoach lines is the world-renowned Wells Fargo, which still operates to this day.

The men who drove these magnificent vehicles must have presented a splendid sight jouncing across the bleak terrain, the driver up top ably controlling his team of six horses. Drivers had to swear an oath of allegiance when carrying the US Mail. All were invariably men, usually under the age of forty. That said, it was only discovered on the death in 1879 of a certain Charley Parkhurst that this driver was actually a woman. During her sixty-seven years, Charlotte had lived life as a man and nobody had ever suspected the truth, such was her ability and tenacity to do a man's job.

It was a tough undertaking that demanded skill as well as strength. Often called 'jehus' (named after an old biblical king of Israel), they were well paid. Driving coaches was a much sought-after job, carrying prestige as well as the responsibility for delivering passengers and goods on time. These men were the kings of the highway, and were often likened to the charioteers of ancient Rome.

When valuable cargo was on board, a shotgun guard sat beside the driver. Otherwise it was the jehu who decided which passenger could have the honour of accompanying him on the front seat. Three pairs of reins were held in the left hand leaving the right hand free for the whip. A skilled driver only used the implement to direct his team, never actually touching them with the snapper. Whips were a prized possession, the handle often being decorated with silver trimming. Effective control of the team meant that gloves were rarely worn. This often led to frostbitten fingers in winter.

Many young men aspired to become a driver on one of the established routes. But this was only possible after learning the craft over a period of years. Controlling the horses and a heavy coach was only part of the job: reliability, responsibility and good time-keeping were all essential requirements that could only be attained through experience.

This story tells how one young man learned a

tough lesson, one that pressed home the brutal truth that driving a stagecoach involved far more than he had ever envisaged.

ONE

TRACE OF BLOOD

'Looks like Cochise has gone on vacation,' the driver commented to his guard as the stagecoach rumbled through Apache Pass in the Dragoon Mountains. Shotgun Dick Willis merely nodded as hawkish eyes nervously scanned the bleak terrain. It was a sceptical reaction. Not trusting the comment of his associate, Willis clutched the trusty double-barrel Greener tightly across his chest. He was taking no chances of being surprised by the Chiricahua chieftain.

The various Apache tribes scattered throughout southern Arizona lived for their ability to wage war against the white invaders. Cochise was known to resent any intruders passing through his land. But he harboured a particular hatred for Mexicans. Coaches had been attacked before on more than one occasion. It was a dangerous run from Elfrida westward to Tucson, making an armed lookout essential.

10

'I'd trust that critter like I'd hug a sidewinder.' The guard's acidic response elicited a knowing grunt of accord from the driver. Another half hour passed before Trace Wildeblood felt able to relax as the coach dropped down onto the flats below the pass. He had pushed the team of six at a hard pace to get through the broken country where every rock held a potential enemy. They had emerged unscathed much to the discomfort of the passengers, especially the four riding up top who were forced to cling on for dear life.

No complaints were uttered, however. It was a sight better than suffering a gruesome fate at the hands of the ruthless Apache chief. Death at the hands of Apache warriors was a painfully slow process. The low cloud dusting the tops of surrounding hills had lifted as the sun burnt through the grey pall.

'You can relax now, folks,' Trace called out, slackening his hold on the reins to ease the sweating team down to a steady canter, 'We're through the worst part.' Everybody thankfully could breathe easier. Nervous chatter, silenced as they had negotiated the bleak pass, once again filled the coach.

It was cut short by Trace as he began to sing a popular ditty to express his relief at thwarting Cochise, not to mention pride at being promoted to chief driver for the Pima County branch of the Southern Overland Stage Line. Every driver was well aware that safety of passengers and cargo was a number one priority. And Trace had achieved an enviable reputation among his contemporaries.

'We've escaped the clutches of that blamed redskin, Trace,' Shotgun Willis grumbled good naturedly, 'Do we now have to suffer another of your darned renditions? What d'yuh reckon, folks?' he appealed with a laugh to the passengers. Light-hearted mockery floated out of the open windows. It had to be said that Trace Wildeblood was no song-ster. His tuneless efforts could easily be compared to the mournful howl of a coyote in pain.

'You jaspers don't appreciate good music,' he snorted but nevertheless desisted from any further assault on sensitive eardrums. 'Reckon we should be in Tucson by three on the dot at this rate. Then I can sing all I want lying in a hot bath out back of Shorty Dunne's barber shop.'

He was about to continue his dialogue when a rifle shot lifted the hat from one of the passengers. The four men sitting up top, none of whom were armed, immediately shrank down behind the luggage. 'Looks like road agents,' Willis shouted above the thundering pound of four-and-twenty hoofbeats. 'Whip 'em up to full gallop, Trace, while I keep the thieving critters busy.'

Six ambushers had suddenly emerged from hiding as the coach rattled past a cluster of boulders. More gunfire from hand guns clipped the edge of the coach, sending slivers of wood flying into the air. 'Brad Metzler ain't gonna be too pleased at having one of his prize Concords chewed up,' Trace commented acidly, while keeping his head down.

But hitting a target while controlling a horse is difficult at the best of times. Trace hunkered down while urging the team on with skilled dexterity. The well-trained horses immediately picked up the pace, sensing the danger closing in from behind. One bravura roof passenger curious to see what kind of danger had been thrust upon them, foolishly raised his head above the parapet. Half his right ear dissolved in a splay of red. 'Aaaaaagh!' The scream of pain saw him disappear from view, moaning but still clinging on for dear life to the steel luggage rack.

'Keep your heads down,' Willis shouted rather too late for that unfortunate passenger. 'The next shot might blow your head off.' Then to the inside passengers, 'If'n anybody down there has a gun, let's see you using it. These guys mean business.' One barrel of the shotgun aimed at the nearest masked brigand produced a large red splatter across the skunk's chest, punching him out of the saddle. 'Yee hah!!' the shotgun rider gleefully yammered. 'One down five to go.'

Dick Willis, like his pard, was a highly experienced stagecoach guard. But this was not one of his regular runs. The only reason he was on this journey was due to a transfer he was making, to the southern run between Tucson and Nogales on the Mexican border. Trace gave a silent prayer of thanks that he was present on this particular journey. The second barrel of the shotgun was equally devastating. This time it was Wildeblood who emitted a cutting bellow of exhilaration. 'Geez, Dick, these fellas must be greenhorns, coming at us from the rear like that,' he breathlessly commented. 'Any bushwhacker worth his salt would have blocked the trail up front.'

But the coachmen did not have things all their own way. One of the passengers, leaning out too far to obtain a good shot, was chopped down by a .45 slug. The spine-chilling gurgling in the poor wretch's throat was too much for the glove salesman sitting beside the victim. Goggling at the poor sap hanging over the window like a rag doll made him heave up his last meal. Blood dribbled down the coachwork before one of the others managed to haul him back inside. The awful stench mingling with that of death was barely heeded. The brutal death was enough to prevent any further assistance from the two remaining passengers. Both were scared stiff, being unused to this degree of violence at such close quarters.

With the guard's shotgun now empty, Trace handed over his own Winchester rifle. 'Use this, Dick. The team can't keep up this speed for much longer.' Already the horses were beginning to flag. Galloping at full pelt was only possible for short distances, especially under a burning Arizona sun. But the lever action repeater soon encouraged the bandits to call off their attempted robbery. A few haphazard shots to register their annoyance and to save face saw them drop back to collect the two bodies of their dead sidekicks.

Trace was buzzing with ill-concealed delight at having thwarted the robbery. His colleague was no less enthused. Both men promised to meet up once they reached Tucson and celebrate with a few drinks. The pace of the team slackened to a steady trot, enabling the winded animals to regain their vigour. An unscheduled stop was made at the Saguaro trading post to check the damage to goods and people, not to mention some much needed refreshment following the unsettling episode.

The dead man was left with the trading post manager for later collection by the Tucson undertaker. After the injured passenger's bleeding ear had been bandaged and the horses allowed to cool down and slake their thirst, the journey continued apace. Trace was well aware they needed to pick up speed so as to arrive at the stage depot in Tucson on time.

Brad Metzler the superintendent was a stickler for punctuality, and not even an attempted hold-up would cut much ice with him. The guy was even known to deduct the pay of late arrivals. That said, he ran the most efficient stagecoach service in the territory. A hard taskmaster there was no denying, but the pay was good and drivers were queuing up to work for him.

Shotgun took out his pocket watch to check the time. 'Keep to this pace and we should arrive five minutes early. Old Metzler won't have any chance to moan at us then.' He smiled as a roadrunner scooted alongside the coach trying to outrun the Concord.

'That'll fox the critter,' Trace replied. 'I might even ask him to give us a bonus.'

Willis grunted. 'Fat chance of that happening. The guy's fist is tighter than Milly Minx's corsets.' Both men chuckled uproariously. The lady in question was the most popular of the soiled doves at Canary Jane's Hen House. Dick pointed to a swirl of dust up ahead. 'Ain't that the mud wagon from Benson?'

They quickly overhauled the small celerity coach pulled by two mules. It was used to deliver and collect the regular mail and trade goods from local farms in the Tucson area. The disparaging nickname had been given to the rickety coach by Concord drivers. Unfortunately for those who drove them the name, like mud, had stuck.

This particular driver was a young sprog called Jeff Hayden. He was accompanied by a lone passenger. The old jigger was snoozing in the back, jammed between a clutch of caged chickens and a delivery of smelly cowhides bound for the tannery. Jeff heaved a sigh of impatience as the large Concord rumbled by. He coughed, covering his face to avoid the cloud of dust churned up by the wheels of the bigger vehicle.

Nevertheless, he acknowledged the driver's enthusiastic greeting with a desultory wave of his own. Trace Wildeblood was his hero. Unlike some of the less sporting drivers, Trace had never looked down on those condemned to operate the celerities. Nothing would have given young Jeff greater satisfaction than being put in charge of a Concord. That was his dream job. Yet all he ever did was lumber about on this heap of junk. He snorted in disgust as Mose Tucker belched loudly in his sleep. The passenger had been taken on by the Catalina saloon in Tucson as a swamper. No wonder they called this cart a mud wagon.

Jeff had been engaged as a driver working the daily schedule between neighbouring settlements encircling Tucson. Like all young men eager for excitement and adventure, he was impatient to move up in the world. And to his mind, sitting atop a Concord was the ultimate accolade. Yet here he was six months later still stuck behind these godarned mules. It wasn't fair. He was good with horses, could handle a whip, and knew all the routes out of Tucson like the back of his hand.

The disgruntled driver mumbled under his breath as the Concord disappeared from view. But the steely glint in his eye showed he was determined to tackle the superintendent on reaching town. It was time he was given a more responsible position with the company. A curled lip greeted another belch from the soused passenger. It was enough for a lurid curse to turn the air blue as Jeff irritably bemoaned his lot.

In the meantime, Trace Wildeblood had arrived in Tucson with five minutes to spare. The superintendent was awaiting his arrival, as ever, a watch in hand. His sour look, however, indicated that he had spotted the ragged edges of his prized Concord. He stepped down to greet the coach as it rumbled to a halt running an accusatory finger along the ragged edges. 'Something happened I should know about, Trace?' he asked in a terse manner, throwing a bleak look towards the driver.

'We were attacked by bandits, Brad,' Trace calmly

explained. 'They jumped us on the flats five miles west of Apache Pass. Shotgun here saw them off. The darned fools tried to overhaul us from behind.' He scoffed. 'Greenhorns if'n you ask me. We stopped at Saguaro. . . .' The breezy clarification was cut short when he remembered the main reason for the impromptu halt. 'One of the passengers was shot dead – God rest his soul. We left him there. Another was injured.' The man in question was clearly identified by the bandage swathing his head as he was helped down off the coach by the guard.

Metzler gulped, his craggy face turning grey. Injured passengers were bad for business. A dead one would need a detailed report sending to the head office in Phoenix. He hurried across to the passenger. 'Take this man to the surgery straightaway, Willis,' he ordered the guard. 'Tell Doc Fisher to send the bill to me. Naturally your ticket money will be reimbursed, sir,' he clucked, ingratiating himself with the man. 'The Southern Overland always looks after its passengers.'

He then turned his attention back to the driver. 'It does you credit to have thwarted those brigands, Trace,' he sparingly praised his top driver. 'But you'll need to have a report of this incident on my desk first thing tomorrow morning.' And with that he dismissed the driver with a wave of his hand and disappeared back into the office.

Once all the luggage and other cargo had been removed and dispersed, Trace drove the coach down to the repair shop at the end of town. It would be out of service for a couple of days, but at least the company had two others that were fully operational. He had agreed to meet Shotgun Willis in the bar of the Fortunado saloon in two hours. Plenty of time to see to the horses and enjoy that much anticipated bath.

More important to the driver than any drink with his buddy was his meet-up with the lovely Sophie Dexter. A change into clean duds would be needed for that liaison. He had been walking out with the owner of the Fortunado for some months. Sophie had arrived in Tucson a year previously with a substantial cash holding that was immediately deposited in the town's only safe at the assay office. Rumours of an inheritance left by a wealthy relative who had made his pile from gold prospecting were neither confirmed nor denied.

Numerous enquiries had been made as to potential business enterprises that could be pursued. None had taken her fancy until Dutch Henry Van der Maas had intimated he wanted to sell up and moved back to his home country. Sophie's interest was kindled at the prospect of running a saloon. More than one eyebrow had been raised when the idea was broached. Women were not meant to engage in such dubious enterprises. Saloons were male-orientated establishments purely for their entertainment. The only females present were doxies and calico queens, those from the lower orders of western society. Could she not run a dress shop? Or maybe a candy store?

19

Such suggestions edged with barely concealed cynicism and derision were like a red rag to a bull where Sophie Dexter was concerned. She immediately settled the problem by agreeing terms with the Dutchman. And here she was nine months down the line having made her mark in a man's world. And with flying colours. The Fortunado was the most successful saloon in Tucson, due primarily to Sophie's unique approach to handling the more raucous of her patrons. A soft touch accompanied by smirking putdowns had worked miracles where the tough approach had previously failed.

Her association with Trace Wildeblood had come about following a trip to Albuquerque in New Mexico to engage the services of an interior designer. The two had been thrown together by circumstance, and romance had blossomed. Their tryst was becoming serious. It had even reached the stage when Trace was seriously considering a proposal of marriage.

TWO

AMBITION THWARTED . . .

An hour after the Overland had arrived, Jeff Hayden was approaching the outlying buildings of Tucson. The town appeared through the heat haze of mid-afternoon, further adding to his sense of disgruntlement. Towering Saguaro cacti reared up as far as the eye could see. Grand monoliths sprouting from the desert where saltbush and teddy bear chollas dominate the arid terrain. A mind-boggling sight indeed for newcomers to the south west.

Yet far from eliciting a proud sentiment of belonging in the young driver, they only served to stir up a simmering resentment, making him ever more eager to press home his claim. His fizzing brain was so engrossed in turning over the best way to approach

21

Brad Metzler that he failed to notice a wagon approaching. It was carrying logs and pulled by a quartet of heavyweight oxen. A pair of teamsters brandishing long whips were guiding the lumbering animals.

At the last minute and warned by a harsh cry from one of the worried teamsters, Jeff heeded the possibility of an imminent collision. He hauled the mules to one side. But this section of the street was too narrow for vehicles to pass with ease. Too late Jeff sensed his predicament. The left rear wheel of the celerity mounted the axle of the heavier wagon. And there it stuck fast, neither vehicle able to move. The whole street became blocked.

'Get that darned heap off'n my wagon, kid,' the nearest teamster shouted angrily.

Behind Jeff the hens were squawking loudly, which jerked the slumbering form of Mose Tucker into bleary-eyed wakefulness. 'Wh-what's h-happening?' he slurred, peering around. 'H-has Cochise attacked?'

Jeff ignored the drink-induced query, concentrating on his own dilemma. Never one to bow down to threats from anyone, yet knowing full well that he was in the wrong, Jeff squared his shoulders, trying to brazen out the error of judgement. 'You should have pulled over,' he blustered, remaining seated. 'Teams on the left have right of passage.' He didn't know if they did or not. It was a fleeting excuse he hoped would pass muster.

The teamster was having none of it. 'You shift that

heap of junk right now or I'll take you apart.' The threat was supported by a back-up driver who now made his presence felt. 'Give the cocky mutt a taste of the lash, Hep,' he gratingly urged his pard. Hep Rennick raised the whip and flicked the long snake of braded cowhide towards the now standing young celerity man. The stroking serpent wrapped itself around Jeff's neck. A quick jerk and he was dragged off the mail coach, plummeting in a heap on to the hard ground.

The heavy tumble knocked the breath from Jeff's lean frame. Crawling about in the dust, the stunned driver attempted to shake the mush from his head. Rennick's whip hand flexed, all set to continue the chastisement. An ugly grin scoured his face as his right arm drew back, holding the whip handle. The deadly lash, wriggling behind like a hungry sidewinder, was all ready to deliver a sizzling cut to the helpless young victim.

But it never happened. Suddenly the whip was dragged from Rennick's grasp. Surprise was writ large across his dirt-smeared visage when he turned around. The end of the whip had been caught by Trace Wildeblood. Slowly and with meaningful deliberation, the Concord driver wound up the whip. And there he stood, straight as a die, the firm posture challenging Rennick to make his play.

The teamster did not disappoint. A growl of antagonism gurgled in his throat as he rushed forwards, his right arm swinging in a wide loop. He was a hefty brute. And had the vicious haymaker landed, Trace would have been instantly removed from the fracas. But the Concord man quickly stepped to one side, slamming the butt end of the whip down on the teamster's head. It was not a stunning blow, but enough to ensure he would not be continuing the fight.

The other man shuffled round the end of the wagon to join his pard, ready to resume the brawl. Only then did he recognize the renowned Concord driver and ex-gunfighter. Jeb Dooley stumbled to a halt. His eyes widened. 'Sorry about that, Mister Wildeblood. My pard's new around here. He didn't mean no harm.'

Trace jammed the coiled whip into the teamster's arms. 'Best you inform your pal of the proper use for this, Jeb,' he muttered barely above a drawled whisper. 'It's a mite safer that way. Next time he won't come off so lightly. Now get that rig moving so that folks can pass about their business.'

Without another word, Dooley hauled his buddy to his feet and quickly extricated both wagons from their impasse. Trace carefully watched the pair of muttering teamsters get on their way while helping the stunned figure of Jeff Hayden to his feet. 'Gee, I'm sure glad you came along, Trace,' the young driver gushed, dusting himself down. 'That critter was all set to flay me alive.'

'You should have been keeping your eye on the job,' the older man intoned, pasting a serious mien on to his weathered features. 'Next time you might not be so fortunate to have me passing by. Some'n on your mind, boy?' He slapped the dust off to make the boy more presentable. 'I'll bet a month's pay it's that gal you're a-courting who waits table at the Jerusalem Diner.'

Jeff shook his head. 'Then you'd lose, Trace.' He was breathing hard following the unsettling incident with the logging crew. His shoulders lifted in a resigned shrug. 'It ain't that at all. Fact is, I'm getting tired of hauling that mud wagon around when I should be driving one of those Concords.' His voice rose in indignation. 'It ain't right, Trace. Old Metzler ought to have seen by now what a good driver I am.' His mouth drooped as they walked across the street to where the superintendent was waiting. The vinegary look aimed at his young employee did not bode well for Jeff's ambition to be upgraded.

'What in thunder were you playing at?' the irate superintendent railed. 'That ain't no way for one of my drivers to act. You could have caused a nasty accident.'

'That wagon was taking up all the street, boss. Them crazy teamsters should have moved over,' Jeff interjected trying to save face. 'Anyway, I was on time, wasn't I?'

Metzler's grim expression effectively poured cold water on Jeff's justification. He lit up his pipe, teeth grinding the stem as he stared hard at the young driver. 'Far as I'm concerned, there ain't no excuse for reckless driving. Another incident like that and you'll be looking for another job,' he snapped, puffing out a plume of smoke and prodding the pipe at his youthful driver. 'Now go check in your delivery and get those mules fed and watered. I don't want to see you again until tomorrow morning. And make darned sure you're ready to leave at first light. You can think yourself lucky if'n I don't dock your pay for that darned fool stunt.'

A sympathetic gaze etched a path across Trace Wildeblood's contours as he stood alongside the irate superintendent, watching the downcast shoulders of the chastised driver as he shuffled away. 'You shouldn't be so hard on the boy, Brad,' the leading hand said in an attempt to offer his support. 'He's a good driver really. Just a mite impulsive at times. All he wants is the chance to prove himself. I was the same at his age.'

Mezler turned a stern face to his top driver. 'That sure ain't the way to gain promotion. And you know it.' Trace couldn't help but agree. He knew the boss was right. 'The kid needs to grow up and realize where his duty lies. This incident only proves that he needs more experience before I can hand him responsibility for a valuable Concord carrying freight and paying passengers.'

He then turned on his heel and went into the office. These drivers didn't realize how much paperwork was involved in running an efficient stage service. He shook his head in exasperation, the waxed moustache quivering in sympathetic accord.

Nursing a simmering resentment at the way he

had been treated, Jeff stuffed his hands in his pockets while dragging his feet across the street. He needed a sympathetic ear to make him feel better. As always when he had finished a job, Jeff headed for the Jerusalem Diner hoping to catch his girl Etta Grace on a break. He was in luck. She was sitting out front drinking a cup of coffee. Etta was an attractive brunette who looked especially fetching in her uniform. But Jeff's mind was on other things.

'You look a mite down in the mouth, Jeff,' she commented, noting her beau's hangdog expression. 'Old Metzler been giving you a hard time?'

He threw a quizzical look at the girl. 'How did you know that?' he queried.

'News travels fast around here. Customers have been talking about that fracas you had with Hep Rennick. That ain't no way to get on in the world.'

Jeff snorted impatiently. 'Not you as well. I came over here for some sympathy, not a lecture on where my duty lies.' He didn't wait for a reply. 'I'm sick and fed up of driving that old heap around. I want a proper job. One with prestige where folks will admire me. And I ain't gonna find that round here. Not while Metzler is in charge.' He stamped around ignoring his girl's anxious frown. 'I hear there are plenty of new stage lines opening up in California.' His dour mood had suddenly lightened. 'Reckon I should head out west. A guy like me ought to be snapped up by some jasper who recognizes good driving when he sees it.'

'So what are you saying?' the girl replied, somewhat alarmed by his bombastic manner. 'Does our relationship mean nothing to you? I figured you thought more of me than that. Clearly I was wrong.' Etta jumped to her feet, intending to go back into the diner.

'I didn't mean it like that, honey,' Jeff bleated, suddenly aware of how cavalier his attitude had appeared. 'Naturally I would want you to come with me. There'll be fancy restaurants in San Francisco where a girl like you could call the shots.' He pulled her to him, kissing her on the lips.

The girl allowed herself to meld into his arms before she gently extricated herself from his embrace. There was no doubt that his beseeching look had softened her heart. 'I ain't sure, Jeff. This is my home. I like it around here.'

'If'n you had any real feelings for me you wouldn't hesitate to follow me,' he countered somewhat petulantly, not wanting to hear any excuses. 'With the extra dough to be made out there we could be married and live in a fine house, wear fancy duds and stroll down the street with folks tipping their hats to us.' More reasons to assuage her resistance followed from the kid's silver tongue. He finished with an ardent plea of understanding. It was accompanied by more loving kisses he was certain would melt her heart in his favour. They always had before when his passion was in full flow. 'All I ask is that you'll think about it.'

Reckoning it was best to quit while he was ahead,

Jeff planted one final kiss on those luscious lips and departed, leaving the girl in a quandary. He was crossing the street when Trace Wildeblood caught him up. He was heading for the Fortunado and that much anticipated drink or three with his buddy Shotgun Willis.

'Don't take what Brad Metzler says too much to heart, Jeff,' he advised laying a friendly arm around the lad's shoulders. 'He's the best superintendent in the territory. And I've known some mighty shady dealers in my time. Brad looks after his employees. He'll see you right. But you need to be patient and bide your time.'

Jeff nodded absently. But he wasn't listening. The impatience of youth was whispering in his ear to quit this berg and seek fame and fortune in a place where the streets were said to be paved with gold. And that was San Francisco in California. The word passed down the line in the form of irregular news sheets had painted an idyllic picture that Jeff found impossible to ignore.

'Nothing ever happens around here,' he grumbled. 'If'n what you say is true, even hold-up merchants can't do the job properly. I bet it wasn't like that when you started out.'

Trace couldn't help but laugh. 'You sure are right there, boy!' Here was a good chance to launch into one of the stories he often told when the drinks were flowing. 'One time me and our fine marshal of Tucson were in a posse chasing after a bunch of roughnecks who had robbed the bank in Alamagordo over in New Mexico territory.' He lit up a cigar and blew out a plume of smoke before continuing. 'Those boys had stolen an army payroll before shooting up the town leaving four dead bodies behind. We sure had a fight on our hands that day.' He paused to recollect the incident. 'They led us a merry dance and no mistake.'

'So what happened?' urged the enthralled listener eager for more.

'We finally cornered the critters in a box canyon. They were trapped, but refused to surrender. Two of our men were wounded so I decided to circle around and come at them from behind.' In the middle of the street, Trace stopped and whipped out his pistol acting the part of a fearless gunfighter. He was thoroughly enjoying the adulation the story had registered on Jeff's awe-inspired face. And there he hunkered down, playing out the role of the dashing hero, a tongue-in-the-cheek pretence greatly at odds with reality. But he couldn't resist trying to impress his young companion.

'Bang! Bang!' he shouted, pretending to fire the gun. 'I'd caught 'em on the hop. The skunks went down like skittles. And it was all over before you could say Reach for the Sky.' For a flourishing finale, the alleged hero of the moment blew on the imaginary smoke from the barrel of his gun. He then sniffed imperiously before twirling the six-shooter on his middle finger and slotting it back into its holster. 'So what do you think about that, boy?'

Jeff never got to utter a reply. A slow hand clap from behind cut through the heavily embellished anecdote. 'Don't you be forgetting to tell him it was me who saved your darned hide that day when Texas Bat Straker had you in his sights.' Marshal Calum Crowfoot had been listening in, and now stepped forward to set the record straight. 'You won't be the first to believe everything this guy tells you, boy. He could have earned a good living on the stage as a raconteur.'

Startled by the interruption, Trace quickly recovered his wits. He always had to have the last word. 'Don't you be spoiling the show, Cal,' Trace complained, his lower lip curling into a half smile. 'You might have finished the critter off, but I'd already spotted him. You just saved me a bullet.'

The lawman threw his arms wide, the raised eyebrows lifting towards the cobalt blue sky. 'This guy sure tells a good story. Maybe you should find a publisher and put them all into a series of dime comics, Trace.'

'Maybe I'll try my hand in that direction,' the cocky driver remarked. 'But first there's a drink on the bar of the Fortunado with my name on it. Jeff's gonna join me. How about you, Cal? Fancy rubbing shoulders with a budding author, not to mention the best driver in Arizona?'

'Why not?' was the quizzical reply. 'Just so long as you're paying. Ain't much else going on around here.' Jeff ardently nodded his agreement on that score. The cheerful banter continued apace as they crossed the street and entered the dim interior of the saloon.

The Fortunado was different to many other saloons in that it was kept clean and had been given a woman's touch. Vases of flowers stood on tables with the customary scantily clad painting of a shameless doxie behind the bar replaced by a landscape. That said, the usual array of gaming tables was well established. A saloon without gambling was like a diner without food. Smoke from numerous cigars and quirlies mingled with the tallow lamps hanging above the tables. Sophie's fresh approach had certainly not hindered her profits.

The three men headed for the bar, where Shotgun Willis was already well ensconced. 'Set 'em up, Tiny. And we'll have whiskey chasers to follow,' Trace said breezily, ordering drinks plus another for his pal.

Somewhat remote from his nickname, Tiny Brazos was a hulking six-footer employed by the female owner to keep order. He also had a sharp ear for listening in to conversations. The talk was all about the failed hold-up, with Trace vividly describing the incident to all within earshot. Willis tossed a carefree grin at the marshal as if to say – *Will nobody shut this guy up?* The vibrant driver had gotten round to relating the recent incident on the street when a boy ran into the saloon. 'Hey, marshal,' he called out. 'There's a maverick steer broken into Ma Dempsey's vegetable patch and she wants it shifting.'

'See what I mean,' Cal grunted levering himself off the bar. 'Some days I wish the old days were back when I could enforce the law properly.'

Trace took out his pistol and spun it on his middle finger. 'That was when a six-gun was all a man needed to see him right, eh Cal?'

The lawman held his buddy's flippant gaze with one exerting a more measured intent. 'Those days are gone, Trace. This is what has made life possible for everybody.' He purposefully tapped the tin star on his chest before walking off.

A glib response to the marshal's retort froze on the raconteur's tongue when he spotted Sophie Dexter approaching. She was all dressed up. The fancy outfit was far removed from the usual apparel sported by the saloon owner. Trace was taken aback. 'Goldarned it, Sophie,' he spluttered out. 'Ain't you a sight for sore eyes? You going to a wedding or something?'

'You've hit the nail on the head there, Trace.'

Her paramour was even more perplexed now. 'What in thunderation!' he exclaimed, unheeding of the teasing smile playing with her lips. 'You ain't turning me down afore I've even popped the question, are you Sophie? Who's the lucky guy?'

The woman laughed out loud, giving herself a proud twirl of delight. 'Don't be silly,' she gently chided him. 'I'm just trying on a few outfits to see which is best for my sister's wedding. It takes place the day after tomorrow in Gila Bend. I'm her matron of honour. What do you think of this one?'

Trace emitted a deep sigh of relief. 'Gee, gal, you had me worried there.' He caught hold of her hand and admiringly cast his eye over the costume.

'Anything you wear, honey, will knock 'em dead. Seeing as you're headed north, you'll be one of our passengers on the coach leaving tomorrow at noon, then. And guess what? I'll be driving. Ain't that something? Taking my gal to a wedding. Pity it ain't gonna be mine, 'cos you look the prettiest picture I ever did see.'

This latter aside was issued with a slight hesitation. He didn't want to rush things with this delectable peach. Sophie did not latch on to the rather obvious hint, even though she was delighted that Trace approved of her dress choice. Instead her brow furrowed. 'I thought tomorrow was your day off. How come old Metzler has given you an extra job?'

Trace tapped his nose. 'It's a special run.' His voice lowered to little above a whisper. Not that Trace Wildeblood could ever speak in a low voice. 'We're carrying some valuable cargo. So he needs his top driver to make sure it gets through safely.'

'Hey, Trace,' one of the listening drinkers called out. 'Tell us about that time a wild grizzly attacked the stage in Oak Creek Canyon.' That was all it needed for the garrulous driver to launch into a lurid description of how he saved the day. Sophie couldn't help but laugh as she wandered between the tables chatting to the patrons.

What the overly verbose driver hadn't cottoned on to was that a guy standing close by at the bar had overheard every word. The nondescript listener suppressed a grim smile. A valuable cargo could only mean one thing: gold! It was well known throughout

Pima County that the Oracle Mining Company had struck paydirt. This must be their first transfer to the bank in Gila Bend.

And the last if'n Squint Rizzo had anything to do with it.

THREE

... AND ATTAINED

An outlaw unknown in Arizona territory, Rizzo had been nursing a beer with hate in his eyes. His stamping ground had been in New Mexico until he had busted out of a holding cell in Silver City, forcing him to flee the territory. Joining up with Mad Bill Brooker had been an act of desperation brought on by near starvation.

All his senses were needed to prevent the anger seething inside his bulky frame from visibly showing. It was his gang that had been thwarted by this blabbermouth of a driver when the gang leader had refused to heed his advice about how to conduct the robbery. If the stupid clown hadn't got himself shot during the calamity, Rizzo would have pulled the trigger himself. With Mad Bill stoking up the fires of hell, Rizzo had taken control.

Declaring his intention to assume leadership of

the gang was an act of sheer bravado. He had correctly surmised that none of the others possessed either the nerve or had the nous to challenge his brazen bid for power. Squint Rizzo was determined to cement his kudos with the others by ensuring that with the next job they would not come away empty handed.

Vengeance was burning deep in Rizzo's black heart to get his own back on the humiliating fiasco of the failed hold-up. The one sensible rule Brooker had insisted on, that of wearing masks, had ensured anonymity. As such Rizzo had been able to visit Tucson without fear of recognition.

The rest of his men were holed up in a blind draw three miles west of Tucson. A lone drifter entering the town would attract far less attention than four hard-boiled jaspers on the prod. And from what this big mouth had just intimated, his opportunity had come along much quicker than expected. The cocky dupe had even been discussing the proposed transfer with the bartender. There was no mention of the cargo itself, but thinly veiled hints left Rizzo in no doubt that gold was involved.

Thoughts of running his itchy fingers through the yellow peril left him drooling into his beer. He moved further back along the bar so as not to draw any unwanted attention to his presence. Just another drifter passing through, anonymous and unheeded. And that was how he preferred it. Most guys in his profession revelled in the notoriety that lawless endeavours conjured up. And an equal number had ended their days on Boot Hill. Squint Rizzo was far more astute.

Ten years had passed since the end of the Civil War when he had opted to follow Foxy George Maddox, figuring the blue belly instigators of the brutal conflict had an obligation to pay reparations in the form of Union bank funds. Unfortunately Maddox had attracted too much attention from the authorities due to his flamboyant appearance. Rizzo had no wish to end up as target practice for peacock shooters, and accordingly had struck out on his ownsome.

Union targets of his lawless activities had soon become universal, with anybody being regarded as fair prey. A decade later and still alive and kicking, he had now become the leader of his own gang, and eager for more profitable adventures. And here was the most lucrative so far, being offered on a plate.

After that big mouth had left the saloon, Rizzo exercised his unique talents in persuasion by tricking the bartender into revealing the details of the following day's special Overland run. Shocked surprise at the enormity of the valuable consignment was concealed by a well-honed poker face. Inside, however, Rizzo's guts were churning with excitement. Carry off this job successfully and he would be sct up for a good long spell.

The outlaw departed soon after and headed back to the hideout where his men were waiting. He had no intention of revealing the value of the large gold shipment. The crafty brigand had his own agenda regarding the bulk of the intended haul. Mounting up, he swung his cayuse around, passing the object of his new-found information who was crossing the street. Trace sauntered within feet of the outlaw without any hint of recognition. A twisted look of appreciation at the inane blabbermouth went unheeded as Rizzo continued on his way. His devious mind was already sussing out the best way to grab the loot, and just as importantly, how to escape with it.

The following day, the Special to Gila Bend was due to leave in two hours. An early downpour had left the street muddy and full of dirty puddles. Folks crossing from one side to the other had to wend a tortuous course to avoid them. Thankfully the sun had driven off the dark clouds, and already steam was rising from the ground. It would be another hot one. Hopefully the soft going caused by the brief yet heavy deluge would not slow them up. Time was of the essence, particularly with this delivery.

Trace left the Overland office with the superintendent still in a quandary as to who was going to drive the coach. With Dick Willis already on his way south to Nogales, Trace had offered to ride shotgun. That still meant Metzler had to find a reliable driver. Regular runs did not always need a guard. But this was definitely no ordinary trip. With all the other guys otherwise engaged on their own runs, he had reluctantly come to the conclusion that asking old

Wilko Verde to handle the leathers was unavoidable. Trace would be a solid back-up in his old job of riding shotgun.

The old jehu had been given the job of handyman for safety reasons because he was due for retirement. Always one to look after loyal staff, Brad Metzler had insisted that head office pay the old timer his regular driver's rate. The superintendent could only pray that nothing happened to prevent the gold shipment and its lone female passenger from reaching their destination safely.

Trace was heading back to his room at the National Hotel to get his travel bag together when he was intercepted by Etta Grace. The young woman poured out her anguish to the older man regarding her beau's reckless intention to leave Tucson. Although his young associate's hot-headed stand-point was well known to the driver, he had not figured it had gone this far. But he was a mite loath to get involved in matters of the heart. If'n Jeff wanted to go find his destiny elsewhere, that was his business.

The girl immediately perceived Trace's reluctance to get drawn into a personal entanglement. 'Why don't you get Marshal Crowfoot to talk to him?' he suggested.

The girl shook her head. 'Jeff looks up to you,' she pressed. 'He'll listen to your opinion. The marshal will just lecture him, and Jeff don't like that. I think he's making a bad mistake leaving here. And I'd count it as a personal favour if'n you could intervene.'

Always one to be swayed by the entreaties of a pretty face, Trace hedged some before acceding to her wishes, declaring, 'How can a guy turn down such a heartfelt plea for help! I'll do what I can. But I can't promise anything. Jeff is a stubborn critter. Reckon he must get that from me.'

'Anything you can do would be much appreciated, Mister Wildeblood,' she said, squeezing his arm.

As he mulled over the girl's request, Trace knew there was only one way to make Jeff Hayden stick around. So he headed over to the Overland office where Brad Metzler was checking the inventory for that day's special run. Carrying such a valuable cargo was the greatest responsibility thrust on his shoulders. And it showed on the heavily furrowed brow and anxious regard being aimed at the manifest schedule.

'You found me a driver for the run tomorrow yet?' Trace asked the worried superintendent.

'The only man available is Wilko Verde, and he's due for retirement,' the agitated guy snapped back. He had almost chewed through the stem of his pipe. 'But I'm mightily averse to sending an old dude like that on such an important mission.'

Trace perched himself on the edge of the desk. Only a guy of his standing would have the gall, and be allowed, to act so boldly. Metzler barely noticed the audacious effrontery. All his attention was focused on the problem that had to be solved, and quickly. 'But there ain't nobody else available at such short notice,' the disconsolate official grunted.

'Reckon it's gonna have to be Wilko taking the reins.'

'Reckon I could have the answer to your problem, boss,' Trace said in a quiet voice. Metzler looked up from the ledger he was studying, a faint hope registering on the careworn features. 'Why not give young Jeff his chance to show what he's made of? Even though we both know he lacks experience, he's a good driver, and keen as mustard. With me riding shotgun I can make sure he don't do anything stupid. It's the only choice open if'n that cargo is gonna leave here on time.' He paused to allow the import of his suggestion to sink in. 'I don't figure you have any choice.'

After some minutes of concentrated thought, Metzler nodded. 'Guess you're right, Trace. OK, get the kid over here pronto and I'll fill him in about what's expected.'

'Already done it, boss. He's outside waiting right now.'

The superintendent couldn't resist a wry smirk. 'You knew all along I'd have to accept, didn't you?' Trace merely shrugged. 'Makes sense, though.' Then he called out. 'You can come in now, Jeff.'

The young driver tentatively opened the door. He was accompanied by old Verde.

Jeff clutched his hat tightly in both hands as he cautiously entered the hallowed domain. Metzler aimed a deliberately stern look his way, puffing hard on his pipe before posing the offer. 'Guess you've already figured out why you're here, Jeff. Trace reckons I should give you a chance. So do you think you can handle a full-blown Concord on this special mission?'

The boy's face lit up. 'That's all I've ever wanted, boss. You won't regret it, I promise. And I'll make sure that coach reaches its destination in double-quick time.'

The thunderous look etched on the super's face told the young driver he had said the wrong thing. Metzler slammed a bunched fist on the desk. 'This ain't no race, boy. I want a driver who can keep to a schedule and has the safety of goods and passengers as his number one priority, not some crazy notion of creating a speed record. Maybe you ain't the guy to do this after all.' He then turned his attention to Verde. 'What do you reckon, Wilko? Can this young sprout handle the Special?'

The old-timer thought for a moment. 'The boy sure knows his way around horses, boss. If'n it were me making the decisions I'd sure give him the chance.'

'I agree with Wilko. The boy knows what's expected of him, Brad,' Trace quickly butted in. 'He's just excited at you giving him the chance of a lifetime to prove he has the understanding and good judgement to do a good job. Ain't that right, Jeff?'

'It sure is, Mister Metzler, sir,' he blurted out. 'I can handle a full team and know where my duty lies. You can depend on me. I guarantee it.'

Metzler simmered down. 'It's a good job Trace is going along to make sure you do.'

'How about letting Wilko go along as an extra

passenger?' Trace added. 'He don't have to do any driving, just be there as back-up.'

For the first time in twenty-four hours, Brad Metzler sat back and relaxed. A grateful smile significantly altered the dour look normally reserved for his employees. 'A successful run, and this could be the beginning of a major contract from the Oracle Mining Company. And you'll get that promotion you want,' he added for Jeff's benefit. 'So here's what you have to do.'

He went on to explain the schedule in detail. It was a direct run to the relay station at Ventana Rim, followed by a steady climb over the Sand Tank mountain range through Concho Gap, then a slow descent around the edge of the Sonora Desert, finishing up at Gila Bend. 'Keep to the schedule and you should be there by three o'clock in the morning. The agent will be expecting you. Understand all that?' Jeff nodded eagerly. He couldn't wait to get going. 'Right, well go get yourselves ready.' He took out his watch and flicked open the cover. 'You pull out in one hour.'

Prior to departure, Trace had one last call to make. He entered the saddler's store and headed for the array of whips hanging on a rack at the rear. A large selection were on display, from the simplest rawhide quirt to a magnificent eighteen-foot bullwhip beloved by freight hauliers. In between was a variety of different types for controlling single horse buggies to that which Trace sought – a twelve-footer to control a Concord team of six. He chose one, the

44

handle of which was adorned with silver and turquoise decoration. A fine accoutrement for the newly enlisted Concord driver.

FOUR

CATASTROPHE

Ten minutes to the noon hour saw Trace Wildeblood escorting his sweetheart to the waiting stagecoach. Once this job was completed and Sophie was back in Tucson, he had every intention of popping the question. A suitable plot had even been chosen on which to build a marriage home. The smitten jehu carefully steered her around the various remaining mud holes. Wilko Verde then helped the lone passenger up into the coach before joining her.

The valuable cargo had secretly been loaded into the rear boot. Brad Metzler emerged from the office, giving his new Concord driver a few last minute instructions. Jeff was grinning from ear to ear when his lady friend bustled up to wish him 'bon voyage'. The boy was about to climb up top when Trace stopped him. 'Can't have a top driver controlling these fine horses with an old whip like that,' he said, snatching the ancient leather out of Jeff's hand. 'This one will do the job much better.'

An awestruck look passed across Jeff's face as his mesmerized peepers fastened on to the fine workmanship. 'Gee, Trace, you shouldn't have,' he burbled, stroking the ornate handle.

'A real driver is only as good as the tools he uses,' he breezed, tossing the old whip aside. 'Now let's get started. We don't want to give the boss any reason to tick us off for lateness, do we?'

'You boys ready?' the superintendent called out, studying the watch in his hand. Nods all round saw him imparting the customary starting call. 'OK then... whip 'em up and move 'em out!' A crack of the new lash above the heads of the leading pair found the heavy vehicle pulling out on its vital journey to the bank at Gila Bend. It was also the town where Sophie Dexter was to be maid-of-honour at her sister's wedding to a local businessman. Everybody on board the coach was in high spirits.

Trace's attempt to enhance the jovial mood with a ruinous refrain of 'Home on the Range' was soon cut short by numerous howls of protest. No offence was taken, such was the vibrant camaraderie encompassing both the single passenger and the three Overland employees. Sophie was looking forward to the wedding, while Trace was hoping that its effect would rub off on the woman and encourage her to be more likely to accept his own proposal. Beside him, young Hayden was thoroughly enthused at being given this opportunity to make a positive impression. And old Wilko was pleased to have been given a supporting role.

Nobody therefore paid any heed to the man leaning against a veranda post outside the saloon, nor that he was giving critical attention to this particular departure. Once the coach had bounced off down the street, Squint Rizzo mounted up and headed off to join the rest of his gang. A previous arrangement had been made for him to join them on the southern edge of the Ironwood Forest. From there they would cut across country to arrive at the Ventana Rim relay station ahead of the stagecoach, which was forced to take the longer route.

Squint already knew there were only two men running the stop-over. An hour before the coach was due in, Rizzo reached the station alone. Adopting an easy-going nonchalance he cantered up to the manager who was mending a fence by the corral. The brigand had deliberately waited until both men were outside before making his casual approach.

'Mind if'n I step down and water my horse?' he asked.

'Sure thing, mister,' Ezra Pond replied. 'The well's over yonder.'

As soon as the man looked away to continue with his task, Rizzo drew his revolver. 'Unfasten your gun belt, then raise your hands,' he rasped. 'And don't make any false moves if'n you want to see tomorrow's dawn.'

The pointing shooter saw Pond immediately complying. 'There ain't no coach due through here today, if'n that's what you're after,' he grunted in a less than appeasing manner.

'That's where you're wrong, pilgrim,' Rizzo smirked. 'A special is due to stop here in about thirty minutes carrying a special load that I intend grabbing.' The stable hand was standing to one side. Figuring the robber's attention was concentrated on his boss, Israel Glamp made a dash for the station building. A mistake that cost him dear. Without even looking in his direction, Rizzo's gun swung and pumped two bullets into the fleeing helper. Both were killing shots that struck poor Israel in the back.

The gunfire was enough to summon the rest of the gang. 'Get that dumbcluck out of sight, Larsson,' he brusquely ordered the blond-haired Swedish outlaw who was closest to the dead man. 'The rest of you hog tie and gag this jasper and stick him in the barn. Then we'll spread out and wait for the coach. Those fools are gonna get the shock of their lives.'

'It will help us avenge the killing of Big Bill,' a stocky Mexican snapped out.

'That clown deserved all he got,' Rizzo quickly interjected with a snarl. A jabbing finger prodded the speaker in the chest. 'And don't you forget it, Miguel. We ought never to have attacked that coach from the rear. Brooker was asking for a bullet in the guts. I'm bossing this outfit now, so we do things properly.' The finger then prodded his own chest evocatively. 'My way. You OK with that, *muchacho*?'

The Mexican shrugged. He was no leader, but had always looked up to the dead outlaw after Bill

Brooker had helped him out of a tight spot down in Sonora. 'S-sure I am, Squint,' he stuttered, recoiling under the flickering gaze of the twitchy-fingered hardcase. 'You right, *patron*. Big Bill, he not thinking straight.' He tapped his head in agreement.

Satisfied he had firmly established his standing, Rizzo gave a curt nod. The sharp retort had been for everybody's benefit. He knew that guys like this respected a leader who displayed a ruthless streak. If'n things went awry, none of them would hesitate to put a bullet in his back. That said, he was astute enough to know that keeping them on side was essential to gaining their allegiance.

A leery half smile followed. 'Don't be forgetting that a shareout from this heist will set us all up on Easy Street. Plenty of willing *señoritas* for you then, eh Miguel?'

That thought certainly made the greaser forget any misplaced loyalty to his dead leader. A lascivious tongue licked his thick lips. 'That ees almost as good as all those Americano dollars to spend,' he intoned, grinning.

'No chance of those perty dames servicing an ugly cuss like you, Miguel,' the fourth outlaw, a tough jasper called Chinstrap Chuck Wesker, remarked, nudging the Swede in the ribs. 'All they're after are those greenbacks in your pocket.' Both men sniggered at the Mexican's wretched look.

'This ain't no time for backchat,' Rizzo intervened. 'We've got work to do. So get to it, sharpish. That coach will be here soon. And remember, no shooting until I give the word.'

Fifteen minutes later the rumble of the approaching stagecoach cut through the tense silence enveloping the relay station. Two men sitting atop the Concord were clearly visible to the waiting outlaws. One was holding a shotgun. The driver applied his foot to the brake, slowly drawing the lumbering coach to a halt.

'That tall jasper with the scattergun was driving the other coach,' Rizzo hissed through gritted teeth. 'I'd recognize that smug bastard's face anywhere. He's the one we need to chop down first. Anyone else is a bonus. But you wait on my say-so. I need a clear shot to make certain he stays down.' The whispered command came from the side of the station where Rizzo and Chinstrap were hunkered down behind some hay bales. Swede Larsson and Miguel were on the far side behind the well.

The stationary coach rocked on its oxhide shock absorbers. Trace allowed the dust to disperse before stepping down. He looked around, a frown of uncertainty clouding the handsome visage. Nothing moved, nobody was around. 'You in there, Ezra?' he called out. But there was no answer.

His whole body tensed. Where was the manager and his assistant? Surely they wouldn't have left the station unattended? There was something wrong here. 'Toss me down that scattergun, Jeff,' he rasped over his shoulder.

'Something bothering you, Trace?' the driver asked.

'Ain't sure yet. You stay up there while I take a look-see.' Wilko Verde had already got out of the coach and was helping Sophie down when Trace snapped: 'You stay inside, Sophie. I'll tell you when it's safe to leave.'

Wilko also sensed the menacing atmosphere emanating from the abandoned station. 'Ezra Pond ain't one for playing games, Trace. You're right to be cautious. It smells darned fishy to me.' His rheumy eyes narrowed, trying to tease out any movement indicating danger was in the offing.

That was the moment all hell broke loose. The first shot fired by Squint Rizzo would have taken Trace's head off if'n he hadn't chosen that instant to bend down behind a fence post. Wilko was not so lucky. The bullet took him full in the chest. The poor sap never knew what hit him. He was dead before his riddled body hit the ground. There would be no restful retirement for Wilko Verde, only a cold and lonely plot in the cemetery.

A lurid curse from Rizzo concealed behind the hay bales cut through the volatile atmosphere, knowing that he'd missed his intended target. 'Let the bastards have it, boys!' he snarled, pumping more shots at his hidden foe. The other three hidden gunmen let rip at the same time. Rifle fire poured across the open ground, hammering into the exposed coach.

Trace hit the ground firing off the twin-barrelled shotgun towards the puffs of smoke. It was a wild shot that merely blew lumps of wood off the side of the well structure. Hugging the ground, he snapped open the sidelock and slotted two new cartridges into the barrels. A quick glance over his shoulder revealed Jeff Hayden levering his Winchester from up on the bench seat. 'Get that darned coach out of here,' the guard rapped out. Without waiting to see that his order had been obeyed he turned back to continue the uneven gun battle.

He was stuck in a difficult position, unable to move without exposing himself to the withering fire of the bushwhackers. His small cache of shotgun cartridges was soon exhausted. He was now left in the unenviable position of using a hand gun alone. When his situation could not get any worse, a cry of pain rang out.

Jeff had been hit. The kid had decided that his hero needed help. No way could he abandon him to the bloody depredations of the hold-up gang. And for that he had paid a price. Now lying on the ground, he was wounded in the side. It was not a life-threatening injury but effectively removed him from any further participation in the death-dealing action.

Trace was fuming. The kid had ignored the one rule that overshadowed all others, namely the protection of passengers and freight. But this was no time for recriminations. The guard was still pinned down. And those jaspers would be extra careful now.

With the element of surprise gone, Rizzo knew he needed to act quickly. 'Keep that critter pinned down,' he ordered Wesker and Larsson. 'Me and Miguel are gonna circle around and grab the loot from behind. Soon as I'm ready, I'll give you a whistle

BACKLASH

to back off and join us back of the barn where the horses are corralled.' He pumped another couple of shots towards the fence where Trace was effectively trapped. 'Then we can skedaddle afore that guy knows what's happened.'

A gesture for Miguel to join him found Rizzo crawling back towards the edge of the station. They gingerly circled around behind the various outbuildings to come at the stationary coach from the rear. The gang leader then removed a knife from its boot sheath. 'You keep me covered while I cut open this cover,' he hissed.

Rizzo then proceeded to rip open the heavy canvas of the boot. In moments the consignment was exposed. The other luggage was tossed aside to expose the large bag carrying the gold. Once opened up, it only took a slight nick in one of the small sacks to expose the glittering yellow contents. A gasp of awe issued from Miguel's open mouth.

Momentarily stunned, both men just stood there, anchored to the spot. Even Rizzo was mesmerized by the sight of all that lovely gold. But only for a moment. 'Help me get this loot on to the pack mule,' he rasped in the staccato accent inherited from a German father. The skunk had ditched him early on in life so the outlaw had adopted the name of his Mexican mother. 'Sooner we're out of here the better.'

The large bag contained four smaller ones, each with five thousand dollars in gold dust and nuggets. While the heavy bag was being draped across the pack animal's back, Rizzo made sure that the other two were keeping that pesky guard occupied before they backed off. Bent low, they retraced their steps. Once clear of the coach, Rizzo placed a couple of fingers in his mouth and whistled. That was the signal for Wesker and Larsson to join them round the back of the barn.

None of the robbers had noticed the young driver lying on the ground. Jeff had managed to drag himself under the bed of the coach where he was intending to continue the fight. But too much blood was leaking from the gash in his side. His gun was stuck out in the open and the wound stung like merry hell. He silently cursed the bad luck preventing him from giving any practical support to the beleaguered Trace Wildeblood. Nor was there anything he could do to prevent the theft of the gold shipment. All he could do was keep quiet and hope the skunks did not spot him.

This was not the way Jeff Hayden's first chance to prove his worth was meant to turn out. A few minutes later, the rumble of hoof beats was enough to tell both driver and guard that the bushwhackers had escaped. Trace jumped to his feet and dashed round the side of the barn. He emptied his revolver at the fleeing brigands but they were well out of hand-gun range. It was in a fit of anger and frustration that, having prevented a robbery a few days before, he had now lost a much more valuable cargo.

Cursing aloud he stumped back to the where the coach was waiting. The horses had barely moved, such was their training to ignore any raucous clamour such as gunfire. A menacing look of anger clouded Wildeblood's face on seeing the dead body of poor old Wilko. It faded to one of woeful sorrow, his head drooping. A flicker of movement in the corner of his eye and the guard swung round, six-gun rising.

'It's only me,' Jeff gasped out as he rose unsteadily to his feet clutching at the haemorrhaging bullet wound. He saw the look of accusation in Wildeblood's incensed gaze. 'I couldn't do nothing to stop them, Trace.'

The boy's injury was ignored as an accusatory finger stabbed at the crestfallen driver. 'Why didn't you get that coach away when I told you?' The question was posed in a measured tone, making it all the more poignant. He didn't wait for an answer. 'Protection of goods and passengers is always the first responsibility of any good driver.'

'I couldn't just leave you here to face those crooks alone,' Jeff countered, anxious not to lose the esteem of this man he admired above all others. 'It'd be like running away.'

'And look where that's gotten us,' was the dispirited response. All the fight had gone out of the older driver turned guard. 'It ain't your fault, Jeff. I blame myself for thinking you had the maturity to handle a job of this importance. Clearly I was wrong.'

The young man just stood there, head bowed. He desperately wanted to find some excuse to vindicate himself. But there was nothing to say. He had failed.

Trace walked over to the coach and opened the door. 'You can come out now, Sophie. Those robbers have gotten what they want. They won't be troubling us again. I'll have to let the marshal know so we can organize a posse to hunt them down.'

That was the moment his whole world came crashing down.

FIVE

MAVERICK

The blood drained from Wildeblood's face. His jawed dropped, a frazzled mind unable to comprehend what he was seeing. Sophie was lying on her side. The fancy blue wedding outfit had been transformed into a red vision from hell. 'No! No!' the guard wailed, stumbling into the coach and gently lifting the woman's drooping head. Her eyes flickered open. He breathed a sigh of relief.

'Don't move, honey,' he croaked, tears dribbling down through the creases of his cheeks. 'I'll soon have a sawbones out here to fix you up.'

Sophie could not hear. Half-closed eyes lifted. 'G-guess I won't be able to m-make that w-wedding after all, T-tr. . . .' Then her head fell forward. The fragment of life that had lingered in the shattered frame had been snuffed out.

Another shriek of total anguish, something akin to

a baying coyote, emanated from the coach. Time ceased to exist for Trace Wildeblood. It seemed like an age passed before he slowly emerged carrying the dead body of his beloved. Without a word, he moved across to the station and went inside, laying her tenderly on the manager's bed. No prayers were offered up. Only a seething hiss of total anguish. Yet deep down a burning fire was growing, a frenzied urge to hunt down the killers who had done this and make them pay.

Any allegiance he had previously expressed about obeying the new law enforcement code enacted by territorial legislation meant nothing any more. Authority vested in the tin stars worn by law officers had no place in Trace Wildeblood's blinkered vision of retribution. Personal vengeance was writ large across the anger-soused face. And nothing and nobody would stand in the way of its fulfilment.

When he finally emerged from the station, the grief-stricken pallor had changed to a feral look of hatred. Jeff Hayden winced. He had never seen his hero in such an all-fired rage before. Bunched fists clutched the Colt revolver as he angrily thumbed fresh shells into the chambers. His mouth was a thin line of determination. Vengeance burned deep within his soul.

Finally, cold eyes lifted, fastening on to the young driver. No more recriminations were foisted on to the man he wanted to blame for causing his world to fall apart. In truth, Trace accepted his own culpability. Arrogance had played its part, the need for approbation. Playing the gun-toting hero to this young guy had turned him into a vain coxcomb. 'I'm going after those skunks,' he hissed, commandeering the rifle that old Wilko would not be needing anymore. 'And I ain't coming back until every last one of them devil worshippers is stoking up the fires of hell.'

Before Jeff could reply, a knocking sound cut through the fetid air. Both men ducked down. It was coming from the stable. 'Follow me, and keep behind,' Trace snapped. 'This could be an ambush to finish us off, so as to leave no witnesses.'

With infinite caution the duo crept over to the stable where the knocking could still be heard. It sure didn't seem to be the skulking actions of bush-whackers. Trace pulled open the door, his gun at the ready, and quickly stepped inside out of the light. What he found was the tethered station manager who had just recovered consciousness. They quickly untied him and sat him on an upturned barrel. Jeff gave him a dipper of water, which the dazed guy gratefully imbibed.

But Trace was much more interested in what the guy could reveal about the robbery. 'You OK to tell us what happened, Ezra?' he rasped heedless of the manager's shaken disposition. 'I want to get after the critters that did this pronto,' he said, sticking a lighted quirly in the manager's mouth. 'Anything you can recall will help me catch them.'

Pond sucked on the thin tube, gathering his thoughts before answering. Spare horses snickered in their stalls, unnerved by all the shooting. 'There were four of them. I remember the leader well,' he explained. 'A mousey jasper, kinda shifty-eyed with a flaming red moustache. I couldn't do nothing to stop them, Trace,' he pleaded. 'The rat caught me off guard claiming he only wanted to water his horse.'

'Don't worry about that, Ezra,' Trace reassured the anxious man, allaying his fears. 'It wasn't your fault. These varmints had it all planned out. Anything else you can remember?'

The manager thought scratching his head. 'Well, he did speak in a funny way, sort of jerky in a foreign accent.'

Before the manager could say any more, Jeff butted in with a fervent assertion. 'I could hear them talking when they took the gold. They didn't see me lying under the coach. All I could see were their boots. But that voice Ezra mentioned, I've heard it before some place,' he insisted racking his brains. 'Can't think where, though.'

'Come on, boy!' Trace urged him. 'This is important.'

Then his face lit up as the nickel dropped. He snapped his fingers. 'Now I remember. He was in the Fortunado. He had a foreign accent. After you left he sidled over to the bar and bought Tiny Brazos a drink. I didn't hear what they were talking about. But he must have gotten all the details he needed.'

'I did hear one of the robbers call him Squint,' Pond interjected.

'Yep, that's it,' Jeff added, eager to regain his

soured standing in his idol's eyes. 'Squint Rizzo. I recall that's how he introduced himself to Tiny. They were acting like best buddies when Rizzo left soon after. I never paid him any mind at the time.'

Fire burned in Trace Wildeblood's flashing eyes, a burning determination to seek revenge for this heinous crime. He couldn't care less about the money now. It was the brutal death of his beloved that occupied all his thoughts. He made a silent vow not to rest until all the perpetrators had been wiped from the face of the earth.

And he would do it alone. No witnesses to crow about justice being in the hands of the law. All that counted now was the vigilante law according to Trace Wildeblood. 'Saddle me up your best horse, Enzo,' he instructed to the station manager. 'And I'd be obliged for some trail grub. I might be gone for a spell.' Eager to help, Pond hustled away.

'You going after these critters then, Trace?' Jeff asked.

'Looks that way, don't it?' was the terse retort as the vigilante walked across to the coach to collect his travel bag.

'Then I'm coming with you,' Jeff declared keeping pace with him.

Trace pulled up abruptly and faced this kid whose naive actions had led to this dire predicament. 'No you ain't! Didn't you hear what I said?' he snapped out. 'I'm doing this alone. Any case, your job, if'n you had forgotten, still stands. And that's to take the coach on to Gila Bend and deliver the rest of the cargo. Then you report the robbery to the authorities. That's what you should have done as soon as those turkeys made their play. You disobeyed the first rule of coach driving. And that ain't easy to forget. You can collect Sophie and Wilko on the way back.'

Again Jeff tried desperately to excuse his actions. 'But I couldn't just leave you there alone to face those killers...'

'I don't matter. The safety of the passengers and freight does.' Trace paused, forcing himself to stay calm. He knew that he shouldn't be blaming the kid. All this was down to him. But he still couldn't refrain from a final barbed judgement. 'Sophie and Wilko are dead. And it's down to your laxity. I ought never to have persuaded Metzler to give you the job. It's my fault all this has happened. And it's my duty to sort it out in the only way possible. Now do as you're damned well told and get that coach on the road.'

It was only then that the blood staining the young driver's shirt caught his attention. He swallowed, a feeling of guilt washing over him. Jeff had tried to protect him and paid a price. 'You OK to drive that rig?' His voice had assumed a note of concern.

'It's only a flesh wound. I'll live.'

Momentarily Trace Wildeblood's face assumed a look of regret. The fractured expression on the older gunfighter's craggy face softened as he laid a comforting hand on the boy's shoulder. 'Ezra will fix up a temporary bandage until you reach Gila Bend. Then just get the job completed, boy,' he intoned sympathetically, 'and hope that Brad Metzler will keep you on the payroll.'

'The horse and grub are ready, Trace.' The manager's summons saw him hurrying off, eager to get started on his quest of retribution. Jeff Hayden was left to mull over the stark reality of what being a Concord driver actually meant. It was a mixture of regret and anxiety that saw him raise a languid hand as Trace mounted up and rode away without looking back. The vengeful rider's bearing was ramrod straight, grit and resolution writ large across his broad back. It was clear as the tall saguaro guarding the station house that he would not return until his bitter pursuit had been completed.

Jeff would have liked nothing more than to accompany him. But that was not going to happen now. He turned away, his beleaguered countenance broadcasting to the world the inner torment overwhelming his whole being.

Due to the unscheduled delay caused by the robbery and its aftermath, the special Overland along with its other cargo did not arrive in Gila Bend until just after midnight the following morning. Jeff had driven all through the night. His injured side ached abominably, but he barely noticed. Reaching his destination was now of paramount importance to try and alleviate the remorse he felt for his part in the debacle at Ventana Rim.

That said, he was still an hour behind schedule. The local superintendent was none too pleased at being kept up all night awaiting a special delivery.

His grumbling was cut short, however, on learning of the robbery. 'Go get Doc Spicer,' he gruffly ordered his assistant. 'He can take a look at you, mister.' The blood stain had spread all across Jeff's side. 'And while we're waiting you can explain what happened.'

The driver slumped down on a chair in the transit office. He was drained. Not only in body. It was guilt at having been the cause of two deaths that was eating him up. A cup of hot coffee and some cinnamon biscuits did little to perk him up. 'So what happened?' the ashen-faced manager asked somewhat tersely, perching himself on the desk. He was already thinking of all the extra paperwork this incident would involve. Not that Henry Fudge lacked sympathy. He was only human. But stagecoach robberies were an ever-present threat that affected company profits. And the buck for any loss rested on his shoulders.

By the time Jeff had finished his explanation, Fudge had already decided to inform the local sheriff so he could organize a posse. 'They can head for the relay station and try to pick up the trail of the robbers from there.' Then he went straight across to the telegraph office to send a message explaining the situation to his opposite number in Tucson. The reply when it came from Brad Metzler would not do anything to help alleviate Jeff's anguish.

The kid winced as the sawbones strapped up his aching wound. 'How is it, Doc?' he asked, gingerly feeling the thick padding around his chest.

'Ain't nothing rest won't cure, son. The bullet just

65

bruised your ribs, but nothing's broken. You'll be sore for a few days, but that's all. A lucky escape I'd say, unlike those poor souls who were shot dead.' The medic was tidying up his things when Fudge returned from his errand.

'Metzler wants to know when you'll be back in Tucson.' Fudge's cool demeanour indicated he would be glad to see the back of this piece of trouble for which he had not asked. 'Is he all right to travel, Doc?'

'Don't see why not,' Spicer replied briskly. 'I'll send the bill to Overland's head office in Phoenix. You just take it easy on the drive back to Tucson, young fella.'

During this somewhat impervious exchange, Jeff had decided on his own course of action. And it certainly did not involve driving the stagecoach back to Tucson. He had already convinced himself that the response he had taken at the time of the robbery was right in his eyes. Running out on a friend, abandoning him to the guns of ruthless desperados, would have been the act of a craven coward. It would have been like having a vivid yellow line painted down your back.

'You can rest up here overnight, then hit the trail at first light.' Jeff bit his lip when the sour-faced agent spoke. Here he was being castigated again for allegedly making the wrong decision. It wasn't right. He was damned if'n he was going to head back for Tucson with his tail between his legs.

'I ain't going back there,' he declared firmly. His

mind was made up. He stood facing the Gila Bend coaching agent, arms crossed and legs akimbo. 'You can get somebody else to drive that coach. I'm joining the posse to go in search of these crooks.'

Fudge huffed and puffed. 'Your boss ain't gonna be too pleased about you shirking your duty.'

'That won't be my problem.' Jeff gave a listless shrug. 'Likelihood is he'll sack me anyway. So I ain't got nothing to lose. And helping to bring in these critters along with their stolen loot could earn me a share of the reward money.' Sombre frown lines that had marred the kid's handsome profile faded as his worried mind homed in on the principal motive for joining the posse. 'But most of all I want to help Trace and redeem myself in his eyes.' The sincere pledge was muttered under his breath.

'If'n that's what you're set on doing, best get out there pronto.' Fudge was annoyed at having to find a driver to take the coach back to Tucson. 'Axel Barron, our sheriff, will be organizing a posse to get after those crooks.'

Jeff checked his Merlin and Hulbert army convertible and set his hat straight. Just handling the old yet eminently serviceable revolver was a stark reminder of its acquisition. Old Wilko Verde had presented him with the gun following his first week driving the mail delivery mud wagon. A lump formed in his throat. Jeff Hayden knew he was at a turning point in his life. He needed to pull himself together. As such he threw off the all-consuming misery that was threatening to swamp his mind.

Determination to redress his tarnished reputation was evident to any close observer as he stamped outside without another word. The posse comprising six men was milling about when the sheriff arrived after giving some instructions to his deputy.

'Can I join your posse?' Jeff asked the lawman.

Sheriff Barron gave the newcomer a thoughtful appraisal. 'Ain't seen you around here before.' The tin star's curt response was more like an accusation. Suspicion was clearly etched across the rugged texture of his grizzled face. 'Why would you be interested in going after a bunch of desperadoes?'

'It's personal,' Jeff snapped back. 'I was driving the coach that was robbed at Ventana Rim. Reckon that should be reason enough for me to join you.' A solidly unyielding gaze held Axel Barron, challenging the lawman to deny his request.

The sheriff was the first to break the impasse. 'Guess if'n anyone has the right to be here it's you,' he acknowledged. 'Take that saddled chestnut over yonder. Then get some sleep. You look like you need it. Tell Tate Farnsworth over at the livery stable that I said for him to give you a bed. And be back here by seven o'clock sharp.'

Jeff visibly relaxed. 'Much obliged, Sheriff. Those rats killed some good friends of mine. I want justice for them more than the recovery of the gold.'

After that the posse split up. With the moon hidden behind a bank of cloud, blackness thick as treacle had the land in a tight grip. This was no time to be chasing after brigands in hostile terrain. Barron knew that the killers would likewise be forced to bed down overnight. So he wasn't worried about them skipping the territory. The following day's pursuit would be a tough undertaking. Each man would need to be sharp as a new pin. These crooks were ruthless and desperate, knowing they had nothing to lose and everything to gain.

Prior to bedding down for the night, Axel Barron had telegraphed a message to Tucson asking Marshal Cal Crowfoot to join the posse at Ventana Rim.

SIX

POSSE IN PURSUIT

The following morning they were approaching the relay station with the sun already beating down from a cloudless azure sky. The hostile storm clouds that had been threatening a downpour overnight had thankfully beaten a hasty retreat eastwards.

Crowfoot was already there, and Ezra Pond had been persuaded to accompany the posse to identify the culprits, though he was reluctant to leave the relay station unmanned. Cal had insisted, calmly allaying the manager's fears by informing him that a livery man would arrive soon to fill in while they were away. He was praying there would be enough time to catch up with the fleeing brigands.

When the posse arrived at the station, Barron informed his associate that he would not be joining the pursuit. 'I'm sure glad you're here, Cal. I need to get back to Gila Bend,' he asserted. 'My deputy is new to the job so I don't want to leave him in charge for too long.'

Cal understood his dilemma. But it still left him a man down. Jeff quickly interposed. 'I'll take his place. Trace is out there on his own and I want to go help him out.'

'Metzler is expecting you back in Tucson,' the lawman said. 'The guy was spitting feathers when I left. He wants the full details about what happened out here.'

'Well, he's gonna have to wait,' the young driver contended vehemently. 'You need another man and I can use a gun.' That was true enough.

Cal shrugged in acceptance. His job was to catch the thieves and recover the stolen gold. What happened between a driver and his boss was none of his concern. 'OK, you're in. While waiting on your arrival, I searched around for any sign. It looks like they're headed for the high country. My guess is they're making south through the Growlers to cross the border into Mexico. So we need to get started pronto. Water your horses and Ezra here will give you some trail grub. Ain't no telling when we'll get back to Tucson.'

Ten minutes later the posse left Ventana Rim and pointed their horses towards the hills. The broken mountain country known as the Growlers lay beyond. Cal knew that should the gang reach that notorious labyrinth of canyons, catching the skunks would be well nigh impossible. It was to their advantage that a change of horses had been possible at the relay

71

station. The gang would be forced to a slower pace riding tired mounts, and Cal was counting on this as a benefit in catching them up.

Riding up front alongside the marshal, Jeff made no mention of his discomforting part in the loss of the gold and its two passengers. It was not something he wanted to advertise, even to a fair-minded lawman like Cal Crowfoot. All he wanted now was to atone for his part in what had happened by playing a significant part in the gang's capture. 'Do you figure they'll hold up in the hills until the heat dies down?' Jeff asked the marshal.

'Could be,' was the evasive reply. 'I've wired all the main towns between Tucson and the border. That means half-a-dozen lawmen will be on the lookout for any suspicious riders heading south. I'm just praying that we catch up with the skunks afore they reach the Growlers. A group of four could hold out there indefinitely until they feel the coast is clear to cross the southern desert.'

Silence gripped the eight riders as they made steady progress across the arid saltbush plateau, where giant saguaros reared up. These mighty slow-growing sentinels are unique to this part of the West. Dried-up arroyos snaked between clumps of mesquite, tamarisk and catclaw, clinging on to life between the rare flash storms. The group soon left the lowlands to enter the hilly terrain cloaked in pinewood forest. And this was where they had their first piece of good fortune.

'Over here!' called a burly freight haulier called

Mule Skinner. He pointed to an abandoned canvas bag lying half hidden in a patch of cholla cacti. 'Looks they must have divided up the loot here.'

'Guess you're right there,' Cal agreed. 'We're gonna have to split up, too. You take three men and follow that draw,' he ordered Skinner. 'We'll go this way and hopefully meet up on the far side of the forest. If'n you spot anything, fire three shots and we'll come a-running.' Skinner nodded indicating for the three nearest men to follow him.

Cal tossed the abandoned sack aside. Leading off in single file, the reduced posse picked a tortuous trail up through the dense phalanx of pine trees. Occasional turrets of fractured rock poked through the verdant cloak. Silence pervaded the enclosed world. Only the sporadic rattle of loose stones assailed the ears as each man concentrated on navigating the rough trail in safety.

Once they reached the higher plateau, the pace quickened, but so did the need for caution. Up here, movement could easily be spotted from far away. That was especially poignant when Jeff spotted a body lying sprawled in the bed of a narrow creek.

They pulled up. Only Marshal Crowfoot dismounted to take a look at the prone figure. It was the Mexican, Miguel. And he was clearly dead. A large pool of dried blood and two bullet wounds in the guy's chest testified to that. Crowfoot dipped a finger into the red gloop. 'This guy ain't been dead more than two hours. We're closing in, boys. Do you recognize him?' he asked Ezra Pond.

'Yep,' was the resolute confirmation. 'He's definitely one of them.'

A quick search of the body revealed no sign of the man's share. Jeff drew the obvious conclusion. 'Looks like Trace got to him after they split up,' he asserted peering around. 'He could be close by.'

Cal considered the thought before replying. 'I reckon the other three are definitely headed for the Growlers.' He pointed to the clear tracks heading up into the high country. 'We've gotten our work cut out if'n they reach that darned rabbit warren.' He spurred off, eager to close the distance.

It was sometime after noon the following day that a sharp-eyed gambler by the name of King Adderley pumped out a warning. 'Over there to the west, Marshal. I spotted movement on that far ridge.' The posse drew to a halt, each man focusing all his attention on the distant rim of the mesa.

'I see him,' Jeff hollered excitedly jabbing his finger towards a fleeing horse. 'A single rider, and he's moving at a fair lick.'

'Maybe he's spotted us as well,' Ezra Pond commented.

Crowfoot's rapid fire appraisal of the problem quickly coalesced into a feasible plan of action. 'From the way he's heading we could cut him off by following this gulch,' the starpacker replied. His vibrant suggestion was meant to infuse a positive boost to the disparate collection of volunteers. But now that the likelihood of gunplay had reared its ugly head, a palpable sense of apprehension was evident in the posse. Only the marshal and young Jeff Hayden displayed any eagerness for getting to grips with the desperado. 'This is it, boys. Looks like we've struck paydirt.'

He dug his spurs into his horse's flank, making the cayuse leap forwards. The others followed. It was now a race against time. Would they manage to run the varmint to ground?

SEVEN

BURNING ISSUE

Twisting and turning between stands of saltbush and cactus, they drove the horses to their limit. After emerging from the gulch on the far side of a line of boulders, it was clear that the lawman's assessment had been correct. The rider was heading their way.

But at that very same moment the fugitive veered off the line of flight. He had clearly eye-balled his pursuers. 'He's making for that bunch of palo verde up yonder,' the marshal enthusiastically observed. 'Let's hope there ain't no escape route on the far side.' He led the posse off in hot pursuit.

It soon became clear that the outlaw's horse was flagging badly. He twisted in the saddle and let fly a couple of pistol shots at his pursuers, more in the cause of slowing them down than with any hope of striking lucky at that distance. On reaching the upper limit of the rising ground where it levelled out on a rocky plateau his luck ran out. The tiring horse stumbled and fell, tipping the rider into the dust. An instinctive fear of capture induced the bandit to scramble to his feet and seek cover among a thick wedge of dry brushwood. But he was no panic-stricken greenhorn and had the wherewithal to grab his rifle first.

The posse dismounted behind a stack of boulders. 'Spread out, boys, and keep your heads down,' Crowfoot advised. 'And remember, I want to take this jasper alive if possible. He can tell us where the others are headed.'

From their position atop the broken plateau, the backdrop of the Growlers could be seen across the intervening sward of rough terrain. Fractured towers of orange sandstone reared up like defensive castle ramparts, blocking easy access to the labyrinth of canyons on the far side. It was clear to Cal Crowfoot that this sucker was headed that way. He had pushed his horse too hard and paid the price. Now he was effectively trapped. The only way out was to surrender or die a fool's death.

And the marshal made sure the brigand knew what his options were. 'You're trapped, fella. No way out unless you're a buzzard. Best to surrender while you can. Do that and I'll see you get full recognition at the trial.'

It was obvious from the start, however, that this guy was not going to submit without a fight. He immediately began firing his rifle to inform the lawman of what he thought of his proposal. Bullets chipped rock close to where the speaker was concealed. 'Come and get me if'n you've got the bottle,' he hollered back. 'I can wait.'

Cal did not reply. He knew what the jasper meant. Wait until dark and he would have a much greater chance of sneaking out unseen. They were stuck there. It was a Mexican stand-off with the advantage now in the outlaw's favour. Some of the others were less inclined to hang around doing nothing, and let fly with their own guns. Smoke from numerous rifles drifted across the battle ground. 'Save your ammo, boys,' Cal shouted out. 'This guy ain't going no place. We can wait him out.' But his assurance lacked conviction.

Jeff Hayden was less patient. 'I say we rush the bastard and get this over with.' He racked back the hammer of the ageing Merlin & Hulbert to full cock, ready to make his move. 'He can't get us all.' None of the others was persuaded to follow his lead. It was the marshal who voiced their obvious concerns.

'Don't be a fool,' he admonished the rash kid. 'He'll chop you down afore you've gone two steps.'

'Well, we can't just sit here twiddling our thumbs all day,' Jeff countered brusquely. 'Every minute we hang around here means Rizzo and his other pard are making good their escape. We gotta do something.'

The kid was right. And once they reached the Growlers, the chase would be over. He'd need an army to search that maze. Rizzo could hold out for months and still escape. It was a dilemma he was unsure how to remedy without futile loss of life.

It was King Adderley who provided the solution. 'What if'n me and Ezra were to sneak round the back of that undergrowth and set it alight,' he advocated. 'The wind's in our favour. Ten minutes of that and he'll be frying.'

Cal's eyes lit up. 'Sounds good to me, King. We'll keep him busy from our side while you crawl round the edge.'

Intermittent shots were aimed at where the bandit was hunkered down to hold his attention. Ten minutes passed before two thin tendrils of smoke wove a twisted path into the air. Soon after the crackle of burning twigs assailed their ears. The watchers tensed as the twin fires steadily combined into a full blown conflagration. 'It can't be long now,' Jeff enthused, eager to continue the main pursuit after Squint Rizzo.

'Stay in there much longer, mister, and you'll turn into an overdone steak,' Cal called out, his voice penetrating the splutter and crackle of the deadly blaze. 'That what you want? My jail sounds a safer bet.'

Moments passed before a rifle was thrown out into the open. 'OK, I give up. Hold your fire.'

'Don't be forgetting the revolver,' Cal rasped. The hand gun was followed by the downcast shape of Chinstrap Chuck Wesker. Cal recognized him from a wanted dodger. He smiled. 'This guy is worth a cool thousand bucks, fellas. And it's dead or alive.' This latter remark was for Wesker's benefit. 'So don't pull any fancy tricks. I sure ain't fussed about bringing you in over a saddle. All I want to know is where Rizzo is headed.'

Head hung low, Chinstrap Wesker stuck out his trademark protrusion. His mouth, however, remained tight shut. He had been forced to surrender, but no way was he going to compound the humiliation by grassing up his buddies. He looked away to avoid the lawman's indomitable regard.

Cal stood facing him. 'So, you gonna spill?' he spat out. The man's mouth tightened further as Cal roughly searched him. He pulled out two small bags, opening one to reveal the prized contents. 'And what have we here?' The sardonic retort caused the watching posse to draw in their collective breath. Gold glittering in the harsh sunlight was a magnetic force few men could resist. Greedy eyes fastened on the dazzling haul.

'I reckon there's about three thousand dollars' worth here.' The brisk calculation accentuated the creases on his forehead as he shook his head. 'If'n each of you critters were given the same reward, and there was twenty thousand on that coach, I'm figuring Rizzo has claimed a giant's share of the booty...' He deliberately screwed up his eyes, working out the gang leader's personal lion's share.

It was Ezra Pond who filled in the answer. 'The marshal's right, fella. You've been well and truly ripped off. Rizzo has run off with eleven big ones.'

'There's only one way to get even, and that's to reveal his destination,' the lawman maintained. But the revelation cast against his boss still had no effect on Chinstrap Wesker's stubborn attitude.

'You'll never get that information out of him with words, Cal.'

The sudden intervention had come from behind the group. They all turned as one to find Trace Wildeblood standing there. 'I heard all the shooting from across the valley and figured you boys must have run one of these skunks to ground.' He casually walked up to the prisoner and stood facing him, toe to toe. 'You gonna tell us which way Rizzo has gone, lunkhead?'

Wesker's face remained inscrutable. Then he said, 'Go stuff yourself. I ain't telling.'

Before he knew what had hit him, Wildeblood's hard fist had connected with the jutting chin. Wesker went down. His assailant immediately grabbed him by the shirt front and hauled him upright. No words were spoken as another brutal hammer blow floored the outlaw, drawing blood from a split lip. The watching posse gasped at the brutal nature of the assault. Even Cal Crowfoot was stunned into immobility by the abruptness of the attack. He could read the killing instinct driving his old friend to finish off this guy.

Before he could intervene, Wildeblood booted the guy in the stomach. He also read the disapproval in his old pal's eyes. 'It's the only thing rats like this understand,' he pressed, bruised fists clenching, all set to continue the assault.

But his brutal tactics had paid off. 'All right, you win,' Wesker croaked, dragging a hand across his

81

broken mouth. 'I'll tell you which route Rizzo is taking.' The feral anger driving Wildeblood's attack remained painted across his snarling face. It was a terrifying sight for the man on the receiving end as he poured out what he knew.

The gang had split up soon after the heist at the point where the posse had discovered the abandoned bag. Each man had then gone his separate way. The only thing Wesker knew for sure was that Squint Rizzo was heading for a pass in the Growler mountains called Papago Gap. Beyond that he had no knowledge, as the terrain disintegrated into a disjointed mass of interconnecting canyons.

Wildeblood's smile was feral in its ferocity. 'You're lying,' he rasped, reaching for the trembling outlaw.

But Cal Crowfoot knew that the guy had surrendered all he knew. 'Leave it, Trace,' he ordered firmly. 'He doesn't know any more.' The lawman held an arm out, preventing his buddy from carrying out any further punishment. 'We'll take him back with us to Tucson. He can stand trial along with his pals once we've caught up with them.'

But Wildeblood was having none of that. 'Why waste time on a trial?' he snapped. 'This rat is guilty. I say we string him up here and now.' This terminal solution met with hesitant muttering from the posse. 'One of you boys get me a rope.'

'There'll be no vigilante law in Pima County while I'm in charge.' Cal's blunt assertion was accompanied by a fixed and immutable look at each member of the posse. 'And that includes you, Trace. He goes back to stand trial.' Both men stood facing one another across an abyss of mistrust now dividing their friendship. The posse stepped back, fearful of being caught in the firing line when the showdown exploded.

Time hung heavy on the high plateau as both men hunkered down. The watchers held their breath, none more so than Chinstrap Wesker whose life was now on the line. Finally Trace Wildeblood relaxed, straightening up. He handed over a bag containing another three thousand dollars' worth of dust.

'This is one more you won't need to bother about. You boys can head back to Tucson if'n you want to,' he said in a flat voice devoid of feeling. 'I'm carrying on towards the Growlers. And I ain't quitting until I have Rizzo slung across his saddle.'

'I'm coming with you, Trace,' Jeff suddenly interjected hurrying across to join his boyhood hero. 'We'll bring him in together.'

'Stay here,' the marshal rasped tersely. 'Your place is with the posse.'

Jeff looked to Wildeblood for support. But he was to be disappointed.

'Cal's right, boy. Your place is here.' And with that he walked across to his horse and mounted up.

As he was passing, Cal signalled for him to haul rein. 'I can't understand you, Trace. This ain't the guy I've known since the war. Why are you so eaten up with hatred?'

'This is all my fault, buddy.' Wildeblood's voice was low, filled with suppressed emotion. 'It was me that persuaded Metzler to hire Jeff for that job. And as a result I failed to keep old Wilko and Sophie safe. So I figure it's up to me to fix things in my own way. Jeff should have driven that coach off at the first hint of trouble. But he stayed to help me out. I ought to have realized he just wasn't ready for that kind of responsibility.' He locked eyes with his pal. Both men understood each other. A brisk nod, then Trace Wildeblood nudged his horse forwards and headed off in the direction of Papago Gap.

Soon after the posse headed off in the opposite direction, back towards Tucson, Jeff nudged his horse alongside Cal. 'Would you really have gone up against Trace in a gunfight?' he asked. His young associate couldn't figure out why the marshal would have been prepared to shoot his friend to save an outlaw and killer.

Cal considered the question before replying. 'Trace Wildeblood is my oldest friend. We've known each other since the war. But he still thinks the answer to every problem can be solved by vigilante law.' The marshal fastened a measured eye on the young posse member, hoping it would strike home. 'He and everybody else toting a shooter has to learn that those days are over. The old West where rough justice solved every problem is dying. And none too soon, I reckon.'

EIGHT

BAITING THE HOOK

After the posse had been disbanded and Chintrap Wesker had been introduced to his new accommodation in the jailhouse, Jeff sauntered across to the Overland office to report in. He was carrying the recovered bags of gold, trusting this would be enough to appease the feisty superintendent. As soon as he entered the dim outer office, he knew from the grim look clouding the office clerk's face that such was not to be the case.

Herby Prescott screwed up his angular features and shook his head. 'Best watch your step, Jeff,' he warned the younger man. 'The boss ain't pleased. He's been stamping around like a bear with a sore head since news of that robbery hit town.'

Jeff swallowed nervously, peering at the closed

85

door. Hesitantly, watched by the clerk, he gave a tremulous knock on the door. 'Come in!' an irate voice snapped out. Once inside the inner sanctum, a glowering expression told the newcomer that he was in for a grilling. 'You're late,' Metzler snarled. 'You should have returned with the coach three days ago. Yet I have to pay off some guy from Gila Bend. Where have you been all this time?'

'I joined the posse with Marshal Crowfoot,' Jeff declared. 'We went after the bandits who robbed the stage at Ventana Rim. With Sophie Dexter and poor old Wilko shot dead, Trace was out of his mind with grief. He abandoned the coach and went off in pursuit. I couldn't leave him to go after them on his ownsome...'

'Your job was to protect the passengers and cargo, and you failed.' The accusation hit Jeff like a slap in the face.

'But I managed to recover some of the stolen gold,' he said, slapping the bags down on the desk. 'Surely that counts for something.'

The angry superintendent just stared at the bags scowling. 'There's still gold worth eleven thousand missing and people dead. If'n you had done your duty none of this would have happened.'

'But I couldn't let Trace face those skunks alone,' Jeff pleaded, hoping for some kind of understanding. But no sympathy showed around Metzler's glowering eyes. 'Trace knew the risks, and what had to be done, unlike you.' His eyes dropped to the papers on his desk. 'The plain fact is, I can't employ a driver who doesn't obey orders. Prescott will give you what pay you're owed.' And that was the end of the matter.

'You ain't sacking me, are you?' Jeff gasped out.

The superintendent raised his head. 'That's exactly what I'm doing. Just be thankful I ain't docked your pay.' Then he went back to his paperwork.

The uncomfortable interview was over. Jeff Hayden was now unemployed, and harbouring a sense of guilt laid down in no uncertain terms by the Overland boss. Ears would be sizzling in no time when news of his shameful behaviour circulated round the small town. So what chance had he of getting another job anytime soon?

He left the room in a daze, absently accepting the pay packet. Out on the street his hangdog expression was clearly visible to passers-by. But Jeff paid them no heed. And as always when he had a gripe, he headed over to the Jerusalem Diner. There he was told that Etta was on her day off. For that he was grateful. At least she would have the time to hear him out, and dole out some much needed compassion and support.

In that respect he was only partially obliged. The subject of Jeff's humiliating fall from public approbation was avoided as she cooked him a meal. But he wasn't hungry, and pushed the food around his plate with that same dejected look clouding his young features.

'Ain't my cooking up to standard?' she asked

rather hesitantly. 'You normally wolf it down and ask for seconds.'

'It ain't that, Etta,' he muttered absently, forking a piece of meat into his mouth. 'The food's fine. It's me. I've been sacked by Metzler for trying to help out a friend. It ain't fair,' he bleated, 'I only did what I thought was right.' If he thought his lady friend would agree, the uncertain cast marring her silken features poured cold water on his expectations. 'I can see what you think. Bad news sure travels fast, don't it?' he grumbled, lowering his head. 'So you think I was wrong as well.' Could his gloomy situation get any worse? 'Of all people I thought that you would understand.'

Not wishing to appear uncaring and indifferent to his predicament, Etta hurried across and placed a comforting arm around his shoulders. 'It's not that. I do understand. But you did have a duty to protect those people. I'm sorry you've lost your job. But in view of the situation, Mister Metzler had no choice.' She hugged him as tears dribbled down his cheeks. 'And it's not all your fault. We're in this together. It was me who persuaded Trace to help you out.'

'So what we gonna do?' Jeff asked holding on to her. The girl's silence told him that in truth the answer could only lie in his own hands. He had gotten himself into this tight spot, so it was his responsibility to find a way through the mire. 'Guess there's no point in feeling sorry for myself. I need to do something to make amends.' He stood up ready to leave. 'So I'd better be going,' he said, giving Etta a sheepish look and hoping for some kind words. 'Reckon I've already overstayed my welcome.'

'No need for that,' the girl purred trying to raise a smile on her beau's glum face. She stroked his cheek, pressing her firm body up against his. The intimation was obvious.

But Jeff was in no mood for the closeness being offered. Neither his mind nor body were able to respond anyway. Mournful apologies poured out of him. They both clung to each other before Jeff prised himself free, promising that things would get better. Soon after, he left Etta's room in the boarding house and went back to the small cabin on the edge of town where he lived. He needed to be alone to try and figure out a way forward.

Sleep was long in coming as he lay on the cot that took up most of the space in the one-roomed shack. The distraught ex-driver listened to the night sounds of hooting owls and the occasional bark from a dog. His churning brain was struggling to reconcile the actions that had led to his fall from grace. Next morning with the sun shining through the window of the cabin, he felt a mite better after dousing his head in cold water. Then he headed over to the marshal's office. Perhaps Cal Crowfoot could help him out.

The front room of the law office was composed of bare plank boards. No carpet or wall adornments, unless you counted the stuffed head of a grizzly shot by the previous incumbent. A scarred desk against one wall was matched by an equally ancient rack on the other containing an array of rifles and shotguns.

These were most certainly not neglected. All of them were cleaned and oiled, ready for instant use.

Tucson's lone administrator of law and order was sitting at his desk studying the latest pile of wanted dodgers. His studied gaze was fixed on the pen drawing of an ugly cuss sporting a luxuriant moustache. Unknown to the depicted outlaw and for the first time in his lawless career, Squint Rizzo now had a bounty on his head.

The marshal knew that he would need some good luck to come his way if'n he was going to flush the killer out from his hideout in the Growlers. But in his view no good could be served just heading back out there and vainly blundering around praying for a lead. It was a stark divergence of opinion from that of his contrary pal Trace Wildeblood.

'What can I do for you?' Cal enquired in a less than enthusiastic manner.

Jeff immediately sensed the antipathy oozing from the lawman. 'I was hoping that you'd give me a chance to prove myself. Metzler reckons I ain't gotten the good sense even to drive a mud wagon any more. He fired me. I only did what I figured was right by Trace.'

'Trace can look after himself. He always has, and he don't need any help from a fresh kid. You knew your duty and ignored it to follow your own narrow take of reasoning.'

'So you're like everybody else around here,' Jeff bleated forlornly. 'I know I done wrong, and I'm sorry. I'd do anything to turn the clock back. Guess it's too late for that now. Maybe I should just leave Tucson. Then folks will be shot of me.' He turned around, his head drooping.

The marshal would have let him go. But a little voice inside his head was reminding him of a similar incident when he had been a young deputy back in Silver City. He had been too eager to meet up with his gal and failed to check that the assay office was secure, allowing a hidden thief to get away with some gold bullion. His boss at the time, Alamo Tad Ratcher, kept the incident quiet, thus saving his job. Never again had Calum Crowfoot put his personal leanings before his legal obligations.

'Hang on there, kid,' he called out. 'Reckon everybody deserves another chance to make good.' Jeff's face lit up as the marshal handed over the much revered tin star. 'One bite at the apple only, Jeff. You savvy? Otherwise you're out.'

'You can count on me, Marshal,' the boy pledged earnestly. 'I won't let you down'

The lawman reached into a drawer and withdrew a pile of posters that had been printed that very day. He pushed them across the desk. The vexed question of how he was going to get them distributed had been taxing his brain. Jeff Hayden was the answer. Although he did not let the kid know that.

'These leaflets need distributing throughout the territory leading back towards the Growlers,' he explained. 'They are asking for news of anybody spotted answering to Squint Rizzo's description. So with any luck some sharp-eyed trapper out there will be able to point us in the right direction to track him down before he breaks out for the border.'

'I'll get on to it right away, boss,' Jeff declared, gathering up the pile. 'I know about many deer runs that lead up into those hills, well off the normal route. Reckon I should be able to cover the whole area in a couple of days of hard travelling.'

'Just watch your ass, Jeff,' the marshal cautioned. 'This jasper is one dangerous fella. He's killed already, and he won't hesitate to add to his total.' He stood up and went across to the gun rack. 'Take one of these new Winchesters, and you can borrow a .44 Remington cartridge revolver. That old cap-and-ball Merlin looks about ready for retirement.'

Jeff didn't need a second bidding. He lovingly fondled the sleek contours of the much revered rifle, testing the balance of the finest repeater around. It was almost worth all the hassle he was getting to find himself in this much esteemed position of deputy marshal. All he had to do now was prove himself worthy of the trust Cal Crowfoot had placed in him.

A somewhat jaundiced eye followed the young deputy as he left the office and mounted up. Cal was hoping that he had done the right thing in placing such responsibility on to those young shoulders. Only time would tell. All he could do now was submit a silent prayer that those posters would generate the information he needed to track Squint Rizzo to his secret lair. At least he knew that the outlaw had not yet broken out of the Growlers and made a dash for the border. No cables had yet been received from the lawmen he had contacted on the far side of the mountains.

As Jeff was passing the Jerusalem Diner, he drew rein and stepped down. A quick glance through the window found him trying to attract Etta's attention. One of the customers pointed out the young man gesticulating on the boardwalk. The red-faced waitress apologized profusely, darting an irate look at her beau.

Five minutes later she appeared round the end of the diner, looking none too pleased. 'What are you doing, embarrassing me like that?' she blustered angrily. 'You'll get me the sack. And then where will we be, with neither of us in work?'

'I'm sorry to have caused you any discomfort, honey,' he confessed ardently, 'but I just had to tell you that I ain't unemployed any longer. I went over to see the marshal, and he's made me his deputy.'

'That's really good, Jeff,' the startled girl enthused. 'I'm so pleased for you. Does that mean you'll be staying in Tucson now?'

'So long as I can do the job properly, I don't have no need to leave.' She threw her arms around his neck. 'I'm off on my first job now to post leaflets around the county to try and flush out that skunk who caused all my problems.'

Etta did not have the heart to tell him that he had brought those on himself by not obeying orders. 'Then make sure you do a good job,' she stressed. 'Marshal Crowfoot has offered you the chance to regain your self-respect. So don't throw it away by thinking you can catch this jasper on your ownsome.'

'Don't you worry about me, honey,' he assured her. 'I've learned my lesson. No deviating from the straight and narrow for Jeff Hayden any more. I ain't so foolhardy as to upset the apple cart now.' And with that he planted a loving kiss on her mouth and departed. And only just in time. He was half way down the street when the disturbed owner of the diner emerged from the front door to see what was keeping his waitress.

Jeff travelled to the foothills of the Growler range, pinning up posters in prominent positions where they might be spotted by the sparse population of trappers that hunted in these upper valleys. He was sorely tempted to press on further and enter one of the numerous narrow canyons that breeched the fractured rock walls of the majestic bulwark. The darkly forbidding portals of bare rock, however, were unnerving to the young deputy.

A shiver raced down his spine at the thought of getting lost amidst such a huge expanse of twisting gorges. Yet at the same time it was mesmeric, magical in its grandiose power, holding the awestruck gaze of the wary watcher in a tight grip. He sat his horse on the edge of a mesa for upwards of fifteen minutes just staring at what seemed like a never-ending world barred to all but a chosen few.

The setting sun threw the frightening landscape into stark relief. Bold colours, shimmering with intensity, presented an ever-changing panorama. As the approach of darkness laid its sinister hand across the terrain, Jeff could readily understand how this brutal terrain had become known as the Growlers. He could almost hear the sleeping leviathan deep within its eerie domain stirring as it sensed another victim close at hand.

Another ripple of dread brought Jeff out of his reverie. This was no place for an uninformed traveller to linger. He quickly concluded that only desperation could have led to the fugitive outlaw stepping over this bleakly menacing threshold. All the posters had been set. Time to turn around and return to the comforting familiarity of Tucson and civilization.

This encounter with the forbidding land mass at close quarters had shaken him to the core. How were they ever going to penetrate such a complex labyrinth and bring Squint Rizzo back to face justice?

NINE

TRAPPER'S CHART

A week passed by after Jeff had returned from his outlandish and deeply personal encounter with the fiendish Growlers. Back into the familiar routine of his new job Jeff soon quenched his initial fear of the outlaw's apparently inaccessible hideout. But he was becoming impatient for something to happen. Then a barbed comment by Chuck Wesker raised his hackles.

The prisoner hawked out a disdainful guffaw as he watched the deputy mop out the cell-block floor. 'Doing a saloon swamper's work sure ain't gonna help you catch Squint,' he mocked. 'He's just waiting on the chance to sneak down here and break me out. Then we'll head for Mexico.' A second scornful guffaw followed. 'And here you'll be, sucker, still doing a woman's work while good old Chinstrap will be free as a bird.'

The cutting jibe echoing round the walls of the cellblock was too much for the young deputy. Wesker's spiteful assertion struck a tender nerve. Without thinking he grabbed the bucket of dirty water and flung the scummy contents at the cackling prisoner. The soaking soon choked off the babbling outlaw's ridicule. It also alerted the marshal, who hustled into the block. 'What in blue blazes is going on in here?' he demanded. Seeing the waterlogged prisoner stifled any further comment.

'This crazy kid has lost his marbles,' Wesker complained. 'He needs putting over your knee, marshal, and his backside tanning.'

Crowfoot ignored the sneering whinge. He quickly dragged his young protégé outside into the main office. 'I couldn't help it, boss,' Jeff bleated. 'The rat was goading me fit to bust and I just lost it.' He didn't wait for a response, and hurried on: 'I appreciate that you took me on when every other hand in town was against me. But I'm just itching to get after that skunk.'

The stern look faded from Cal Crowfoot's craggy face, as did the reprimand hovering on his lips. He felt some sympathy for the kid's jumpiness. 'Just going off into those mountains ain't gonna get us anywhere except lost, Jeff,' he calmly explained. 'It's like fishing for that big pike down in Altar Wash. You just have to bait your hook and wait for a bite. Soon as you feel a drag on that line, haul the critter in. That's what we have to do. Keep a cool head and steady nerves. Those posters will jog somebody's memory soon enough. Until then we gotta be patient. You understand what I'm saying, boy?'

'Guess so.' Jeff shuffled his feet, regretting his flare-up. 'I sure am sorry for losing my rag,' he apologized rather awkwardly.

'It's me that should be apologizing for making you do that kind of work.' Cal took out a bunch of wanted dodgers from a drawer. 'You deserve better. So I want you to check these against the list of felons I received from head office in Phoenix. Go through them and remove the critters who have already been caught and tried. Meanwhile, I've got me some unpaid rents to chase up.' A smile of encouragement and a pat on the shoulder saw Jeff setting about the task with a more positive attitude. 'And you can let that skunk in there drip dry. That'll teach him not to make fun of my deputy.' Then he left, with the sardonic parting remark: 'Since you joined me, it's all go in Tucson, Jeff. Never a dull moment.'

The alleged monotony of Jeff's duties was brought to a sudden end the next morning when a visitor from upcountry walked into the law office. And he was carrying a copy of the poster.

It was the first thing that Cal noticed, and his eyes lit up. At last it seemed his ploy had born fruit. Unfortunately he stood up rather too quickly for the rough-haired grey wolfhound accompanying the man.

The dog bared its teeth, clearly regarding the lawman as a threat to its master. The visitor casually laid a hand on the dog's arched back and gave him a stick of jerky to chew on. In little more than a whisper he uttered the magic words: 'Friend, Mesquite.' The hound immediately settled down on its haunches, the menacing stance abandoned as he eagerly devoured the tasty treat.

'Old Mesquite here gets a mite protective if'n he thinks I'm in danger,' the man croaked out in a voice abraded by too much rough moonshine. 'But he loves jerky. Offer him a lump of prime beef and he turns up his nose. Crazy mutt has no darned taste.' He hawked out a brittle laugh.

'I sure wouldn't want to meet him on a dark night,' Cal responded, making sure to keep his movements slow and easy. He then turned his attention to the visitor. The guy was clearly a fur trapper. Clad in greasy buckskins, the bearded visage could have put him anywhere between forty and sixty. Trapping tended to add years to a man's appearance. Held in his right hand was a Hawken long gun. Cal's envious eyes rested on the old rifle. 'That's a mighty fine gun you have there, mister. Ain't seen the like in a coon's age.'

The man handed the sleek weapon across for Cal's inspection. 'It was owned by my pa and handed down like a family heirloom. These old boys are mighty rare nowadays.'

The marshal lovingly caressed the shiny walnut stock. 'I'd sure like to own one myself,' he conceded, but with a hesitant caveat: '. . . but only for display purposes. A guy in my position has to have a rifle offering much better protection.' He pointed to the row of Winchesters locked in the wall rack. 'Repeaters give much more effective stopping power.'

The trapper was not convinced. 'In the right hands, the Hawken has range, accuracy and reliability on its side. Indians are scared off just by looking at it. And I can fire off five rounds in a minute. And to prove it I'm still here.'

Cal couldn't help but admire the old-timer's logic. 'So what can I do for you, Mister...? he asked, eyeing up the poster.

'The name is Beavertail Hokum. It says here that there's a reward for information concerning some jasper heading up into the Growlers. That the case, marshal?'

Crowfoot sensed an astute brain under the greasy exterior. 'That depends on what you have to offer,' countered the lawman.

'Well, I sure ain't telling unless you pay up,' the trapper shot back. 'And believe me, what I have to tell is worth a heap of dough.'

Cal thought for a moment before playing along with the parley. 'So what do you reckon it's worth, Mister Hokum?'

'I have a cabin up in the hills. Come down into Tucson about once a month for supplies. And I'm thinking that five bucks is a fair price for what I have to sell.' The declaration was delivered in a serious tone of voice.

Cal's eyes lifted momentarily, the glimmer of a

smile passing between him and his deputy. 'What do you think, Jeff? Should we pay the guy?'

Jeff played along, scratching his head in thought. 'You sure strike a hard bargain, Mister Hokum. But I reckon we can just about stretch to five bucks, providing it helps keep the law around here.'

The marshal reached into a drawer of his desk and removed a cash box. He slowly counted out the five silver dollar coins and handed one of them over. 'You'll get the rest when I'm satisfied with what you have to say,' was the measured assertion, delivered with a deadpan frown.

Hokum made a point of testing the coin with his teeth before pocketing his reward. 'A fella stopped at my place offering to buy one of my horses. I got to rearing appaloosas since the beaver trade died,' he added. 'This fella had a loaded mule with him. Said his own horse had tripped and broken a leg. He was heading for Sunset Canyon on the far side of the Dragon's Teeth, where he claimed there was good prospecting. I know that area like the back of my hand. Ain't no gold up there. Only reason any jasper would head that way is to reach Papago Gap. My bet is he's on the run and heading for the Mexican border. He had that mean-eyed look of a desperado.'

Crowfoot tensed. Could this be their man? 'Did the guy have a red moustache?' he snapped out, before quickly settling down as Mesquite raised his head.

The trapper shook his own pate, the beavertail perched on top jiggling playfully. 'But he did have a

101

funny accent. Never heard the like before. Kinda choppy.'

'That's Rizzo all right. He's German, Mister Hokum,' interjected the excited deputy. 'The skunk must have shaved the moustache off. This guy robbed the Overland stage and killed the passengers. You're lucky to be still alive.'

'Didn't give him no call to do me any harm.' Beavertail pulled out an old corncob and chewed on the stem, his ribbed brow crinkling in thought. 'But now I come to think on it, paying me in gold sure fits in with what you've said. And it was from an Oracle bag.'

'That's Rizzo all right,' Cal said.

The grizzled face dropped as another less optimistic notion occurred to the trapper. 'Looks like it was a bum move on my part to point him in the right direction.'

'You weren't to know,' Cal assured the trapper. 'And I sure do appreciate you coming in to tell me this, Mister Hokum. Reckon I'd better be getting after this jasper before he escapes for good.'

'After what you just said, Marshal,' the trapper interjected with a fresh twinkle in his eye, 'I reckon I can help you out there.' He pulled out a well-worn map from his gunnysack and opened it up. A grubby finger pointed out the route taken by the fugitive. 'You'll never catch him following that trail over the Dragon's Teeth. He's gotten too big a start. But go this way along an old Indian trail across the Mammoth Drove Road.' The finger shifted to the east, pointing out a prominent needle of rock labelled The Flagpole.

'Cut left of this and you'll soon hit the Drove. Can't miss all those bones scattered around. Then you'll be able to cut him off at Ponderosa Butte.' A drawing of a towering block indicated the direction to be taken. Beyond it was a lake called the Punch Bowl. 'I wish you luck, marshal. Reckon you're gonna need it. You can return the map when you've caught him.'

Cal smiled. 'I'm obliged to you. That was a good five dollars' worth of information.' He pushed the rest of the payment across the desk.

'Figured it was,' the old trapper said, pocketing his reward. He then tipped his cap. 'Reckon I'll go spend it in that saloon across the street. Drinking moonshine all the time ain't good for the old ticker. A fella needs Scotch whisky to perk him up.' And with that parting shot he made to depart, pausing in the doorway. 'There's one thing I almost forgot. Watch out for the mark of a horse with a snake's head forged in one shoe. It's the signature of a blacksmith I use in Tin Pack over the far side of the Ironwoods.'

Cal stood up, nodding his appreciation as the man left to enjoy his payout.

'I'll get started right away,' he told his deputy. 'Need to go fix up a fresh horse from the livery stable and pack in a week's supply of trail grub.' As he headed for the door, Jeff butted in. 'What about me? Ain't we going after this rat together?'

'Somebody has to stay in Tucson to look after

things while I'm away,' the lawman declared, strapping on his gun belt and selecting a rifle from the gun rack. 'You'll be acting town marshal. It's a big responsibility. Think you can handle it?'

Jeff's face lit up. He hadn't thought of that. Town marshal of Tucson. It sounded good. Etta would be proud of him. He nodded his head vigorously. 'I won't let you down, Cal. All I ever wanted was for somebody to have faith in me. You've given me back my self-respect and I can't thank you enough.'

'Just keep the lid on things until I get back,' the lawman cautioned, hoping he hadn't made a big mistake here. 'And don't get swelled headed and start lording it over folks.'

A day later, having ridden through the night, Cal Crowfoot had reached the cabin where Beavertail Hokum lived. A roughly built shack lay tucked into the side of a towering cliff. To one side a corral held three horses and a mule, grazing on hay left by the trapper. On the other side skins of fox and elk were pinned up on frames drying out. The lawman decided to spend the night in the cabin, which Hokum had made into a comfortable home. Beavertail clearly enjoyed the simple life. And an array of books told of a man who was also well read.

Before he settled down for the night, Cal inspected the horses in the corral. And lo and behold, one of them was sporting that identifying blacksmith's mark mentioned by Beavertail. Now he knew exactly what he was looking for. Back in the cabin, a glass of moonshine packing a hefty wallop enabled the pursuer to enjoy an undisturbed sleep.

Next thing he knew, the crowing of a rooster was announcing the start of a new day. A cold wash in the local creek soon chased away any sleep-induced lassitude. Birds were chirping in the trees, a chipmunk was chasing its mate across the open sward. An idyllic scene to be sure, if'n it weren't for the grim nature of his visit.

After boiling up some fresh coffee and using the trapper's flour to make pancakes, Cal enjoyed a hearty breakfast. He was all ready to continue his journey as the new sun poked its snout above the distant peaks to the east. Grateful for the trapper's hospitality, he left a five-dollar bill on the table.

Although eager to get going, Cal took time out to search for that all-important distinguishing symbol on the shoe. Fifteen minutes were needed to spot the indentation in mud beside the shallow creek that supplied the cabin with its water supply. A whoosh of relief issued from between the lawman's pursed lips. Now that he knew in which direction his quarry was headed, he set off at a brisk trot.

At least it appeared that Trace Wildeblood had not passed this way, otherwise the old trapper would have mentioned it. Cal's stratagem of wait and see appeared to be working. Maybe he could now catch up with Rizzo before Trace's bloodlust for revenge soured their friendship for good.

A fresh sense of urgency found Cal Crowfoot pushing hard into the mountains. In the distance the

Dragon's Teeth beckoned invitingly. White incisors of scarred limestone stark and austere stood proud against the azure backdrop, ever ready and willing to snap at any traveller seeking to challenge their hostile realm.

He had only been riding for half an hour when he came across a major clue that he was on the right trail. The mule had been abandoned. Basic trail gear had been extracted and there was no sign of the missing gold. Rizzo was now on his ownsome with the bulk of the haul. Thankfully he was riding the horse sporting that distinguishing snake-shoe design. Soon after, Cal passed a cave bearing the cold ashes of a fire outside. A brief recce of the inside told him that Rizzo must have used it as his base before making his bid for freedom across the Mexican border.

Cal pushed on, not wishing to linger in the vicinity where his quarry had camped. The next day he rose at dawn. Early mist hovered around the distant peaks. Drifting in the burgeoning heat thermals the soft white skeins challenged beams of sunlight already probing the deep-set valley in which he had camped. Cal's penetrating gaze shifted away towards a side canyon branching right. This was the commencement of the cut-off suggested by Beavertail Hokum.

At this point he abandoned the trail left by Squint Rizzo to follow the trapper's advice. The snake-mark impression pointing towards the Dragon's Teeth proved that the canny trapper's theory was spot on. Old Beavertail obviously knew this country like the back of his hand. Cal's speculation to alert guys like him had paid off.

All he needed to do now was track the skunk down before Trace Wildeblood took the law into his own hands. The murder of his beloved Sophie had hit his old pal harder than a rampant herd of buffalo. Already he had the blood of two outlaws on his hands. Only Cal Crowfoot could now stop him adding the gang leader's scalp to his rebellious tally. As a firm believer that the office he strove to uphold was sacrosanct where law enforcement was concerned, Cal was determined to see justice administered in the manner prescribed by territorial legislation.

Towards the head of the canyon the terrain levelled out into a broad amphitheatre. And there it stood, majestic in all its towering glory. A mighty monolith of red sandstone giving the bold impression of a fiery spout. Awesome in its intensity, the mighty Flagpole was well named. He slowed his pace on passing the noble upsurge, eyes searching beyond for the sinister remnants of the Mammoth's Drove Road. The bleached bones of a once proud herd half-buried in the rocky wasteland were unmistakable. Grey, gnarled and menacing, these dead relics harked back to a distant past long before man walked the earth.

A shiver of dread rippling through the lawman's taut frame made him all the more alert to the danger posed. Not from these macabre vestiges of a dead past, but from a more deadly foe, very much alive.

And one who might well be close at hand. Even now a rifle could be pointing his way.

Searching eyes panned across the bleak terrain towards the surging land mass of Ponderosa Butte. Had he got here in time to cut off the outlaw's escape route? Nothing moved that was alien to this beautiful yet starkly remote backwater amidst the Growler Mountain landmass.

Beyond the Drove Road, the rough ground of broken rocks rose steadily. A tenuous course had to be picked between huge boulders and pine trees. A broken leg here would be catastrophic. According to the trapper's map, there was a lake falling away to the rear of the Butte. Cal was about to set off again when his acute hearing picked up the low snicker from a horse. And it was close by. He paused, six-gun clutched tightly in his right hand. The sound was coming from behind some rocks up ahead. He cautiously dismounted and approached the potential source of danger with trepidation.

TEN

EDGE OF THE
ABYSS

The animal was saddled and on its ownsome. A quick
search revealed the saddle bags had been removed.
The obvious conclusion was that Rizzo had abandoned the horse and taken the gold with him. He
would surely not have taken this apparently inaccessible route unless he knew he was being followed.
The killer must therefore be holed up somewhere
ahead in the rocks just waiting to pick off his pursuer.
Extreme care would be needed from here on if'n he
was to capture the outlaw.

That notion had barely registered when a bullet
slammed into the boulder near his head. Cal dived to
one side, scrambling behind a pile of loose rocks.
Another bullet chipped slivers off his precarious
haven. The crafty weasel had certainly picked his

109

spot carefully. Cal was pinned down, unable to move. Not a situation to inspire confidence of an arrest.

Just when he was figuring to have ridden into a trap, a bullet echoed across the bleak terrain. Instinct kicked in as he ducked out of sight. But it had originated from over to his left. And it had been aimed at the fugitive up on the Butte. The sudden realization struck home that by some fluke of destiny, Trace Wildeblood must have picked up Rizzo's trail from a different direction. Trace had always been the hot one back in the old days when it came to tracking down villains. And here he was yet again, trying to outsmart his old pal.

'That you, Trace?' the lawman called out, not caring if'n their quarry heard the exchange. 'Leave this to the law. I don't need your help to net this fish.'

'No chance, old buddy,' the cogent reply bounced back. 'This skunk is mine. And he's gonna pay the full price. You stay back. I'll even let you claim the reward. All I want is to nail the guy's hide to a tree.' The brusque declaration was accompanied by a couple more shots aimed at the rocky enclave above.

Cal cursed. Trace's actions were harking back to the days of vigilante law when rough justice was dispensed without any thought to the consequences should innocent victims be involved. He shivered at the thought. Thankfully those days were past. Even though Cal was certain Squint Rizzo was guilty, he still intended for him to be arraigned in a fair trial conducted by a legitimate territorial judge. Cal Crowfoot took the wearing of the revered tin star

110

very seriously.

That said, with some reluctance he was glad of Wildeblood's unexpected intervention. He had to admit to himself that he needed help to winkle this slippery jasper out of his shell. On the other hand, he had to get up there fast to prevent his oldest friend forcing the issue by killing Rizzo out of hand.

From where he was secreted, Cal could see the maverick stage driver scrambling up towards the line of rocks marking the apex of Ponderosa Butte. Beyond it lay the hidden expanse of the Punch Bowl. It looked like Rizzo had been backed into a trap, the only way out being a perilous descent of a cliff face. With nothing to lose he would fight tooth and nail to avoid capture.

Bullets continued to rain down from the rocky citadel as the two attackers crept ever closer from different angles. Rizzo knew he was at the point of no return. That was brought home with a vengeance when his rifle clicked on empty. With only a hand gun left he was being forced nearer and nearer to the cliff edge.

'Might as well give up now, Rizzo,' Cal called out. 'Otherwise the only way out for you is a watery grave.'

'It's better than choking out my life on a gallows,' the fugitive hawked back, supporting his refusal with a couple of shots from the revolver. 'So I'll take my chances with the fish, starpacker.'

'You ain't gonna duck out of this by figuring to take a swim, scumbag,' a gravelly voice snarled out. Trace was closer to his quarry than Rizzo had figured.

'Once I've filled your miserable hide with lead, I'll string you up for the buzzards to chew on.' A manic bout of spine-tingling laughter echoed around the rock-strewn arena.

Panic found the killer edging his way down the north rim of the precipitous Butte. For the first fifty feet he was able to follow a twisting gully, but this soon terminated on a flat ledge overlooking the blue spread of the Bowl. He was trapped. The sound of loose stones told him that his pursuer was close behind. Sweat bubbled on the outlaw's brow. Any minute now and the hunter would find him. Flickering peepers searched for a way out of his dilemma. But there was nothing. Not even a tiny crevice for a chipmunk to hide in.

He turned, facing the gully's exit, the revolver cocked and ready for the final showdown. A blurred shadow told Rizzo the moment of confrontation was imminent. The shadow materialized into human form as Trace Wildeblood suddenly appeared. Rizzo fired. But the gun clicked on empty. He was out of ammo. There was only one course of action left open to him.

No thought was given to the fact that he could soon be feeding the fishes. The alternative was a bullet and oblivion at the hands of the hate-filled avenger who had tracked him down. Sucking in a deep breath he ran to the edge of the shelf and launched himself into the open void. Suddenly he was airborne. The wind snatched the hat from his head as legs thrashed and arms flapped, desperate to avoid the deadly mouthful of rocks below.

'Aaaagh!!' A manic scream of fear was ripped from his throat. Down, down, down he plunged, praying to avoid the fast approaching rocky teeth snapping below. For what seemed like an eternity he appeared to hang there, drifting in this alien world betwixt life and death. Any second now and he would hit the calm blue surface, or smash to bits on the rocks.

No further time for macabre reflection was possible as he hit the water, disappearing beneath the icy surface. The shock almost knocked him unconscious. A reflexive desire to survive kicked in as he swam back to the surface, gulping in huge lungfuls of precious air. But the danger was nowhere near over.

A shot rang out from the ledge above. The bullet plucked water inches from his bobbing head. Desperation lent strength to the floundering owl-hooter, who immediately struck out for the shoreline. 'You ain't gonna get away that easily!' The angry shout from Trace Wildeblood was accompanied by two more bullets, one of which struck the thrashing absconder in the shoulder.

Blood poured from the wound, staining the surrounding clear blue water a bright shade of purple. Rizzo's frantic arms ceased as the jolt from the gash stunned his whole body. Luckily for him it was only a flesh wound. Sheer dread of capture and certain death at the hands of this crazed nemesis of doom saw him feverishly struggling towards the shoreline.

Trace snarled out his annoyance at having rushed his shots. He jacked a fresh round into the upper

113

barrel of the Winchester and took careful aim. This time he would hit the guilty skunk dead centre and finish him for good. Only then would he be fully avenged for the murder of his beloved Sophie. His finger tightened on the trigger as the sights picked out the wallowing fish below.

'Don't do it, Trace!' The grim warning came from behind him. Cal Crowfoot had managed to catch up. And just in the nick of time to prevent his friend committing outright murder.

The jehu hesitated, turning around to face his challenger. 'You keep out of this, Cal. That rat is going to pay big time for what he's done.' He then turned back, jamming his rifle back into his shoulder ready to finish the job he had promised to do.

Cal quickly moved up behind him and jabbed the barrel of his pistol into the vigilante's back. 'He's going back to Tucson to face trial,' the lawman hissed in words intended to convey a blunt message. 'Pull that trigger and you're a dead man.' Another jab served to emphasize that his forthright threat was no idle bluff. 'Now drop the rifle.'

Trace turned, slowly. Their eyes met. And he knew his friend would not hesitate to carry out his grim threat. He allowed the gun to slip through his fingers. Cal kicked the rifle away, immediately securing Trace's hand gun. 'I never had you down as a weak-kneed liberal, Cal,' the vigilante sneered. 'Guess I was wrong.'

The lawman gritted his teeth. His lips pursed as he struggled to contain his anger. His reply when it

114

came was measured and calmly delivered, making it all the more cogent. 'Neither you nor anybody else is above the law, Trace. The only one who's gonna play God on my patch is the Man himself. Anybody who takes the law into their own hands is on a slippery slope heading towards chaos and rebellion. Is that what you want for our country?'

Cal continued to hold the other man's hard-eyed gaze. But it was Trace who broke the impasse, looking away first. Not wishing to abandon his friendship, Cal was prepared to offer an olive branch to assuage his pal's humiliating climb-down. 'If'n I return your guns, will you pledge on your honour to help me take this varmint back to town?'

'I'll help you,' Trace eventually conceded grudgingly. 'Just so long as some fancy lawyer don't help him wheedle out of a meeting with the hangman.'

That was enough for the marshal. 'You scout around to locate where he's stashed the rest of the gold while I go pick him up. He can't get far with a bullet in the shoulder.'

A half hour later Cal appeared, pushing the woebegone outlaw before him. He had experienced little difficulty in capturing the unarmed critter once he had scrambled ashore. 'See you caught yourself a drowned rat, Marshal,' Trace declared, pasting a mirthless leer on to his face. 'Pity my bullets didn't finish the job. Still, I'll be booking myself a front seat to watch you swing, *hombre*.'

They made camp for the night in a glade down the back slope of the Butte. Rizzo was securely tied to a tree while a fire was lit and some grub cooked. Over a cup of coffee, Cal suddenly remembered that no mention had been made of the gold. 'Did you manage to find the stash?' he asked his associate. Since the unsettling confrontation on the ledge overlooking the Punch Bowl, their relationship had become somewhat strained. Not hostile exactly, but certainly tense. Cal was still not sure where Wildeblood's loyalties lay.

Both men sat opposite each other chewing on stringy rabbit legs and fried biscuits. The dancing flames lit up their faces as each contemplated the other with caution. Little had been said until Cal broached the subject of the missing gold.

'Ain't managed to find it,' Trace replied. 'But there's one sure way of persuading this varmint to spill the beans.' A nod towards the tethered prisoner was accompanied by a jiggle of the large bowie knife he had surreptitiously placed in the fire. Grasping hold of the bone handle, he removed the red hot blade and stuck it into his tepid mug of coffee. The brown liquid hissed and bubbled. Trace added a spoonful of sugar, then sipped the contents. 'That sure hit the spot,' he remarked, sticking the glittering steel back into the embers of the fire.

Rizzo knew exactly what the jehu was intimating, and his face blanched with fear. 'You ain't g-gonna let him b-burn me are y-you, Marshal?' the terrified outlaw stammered out.

Cal Crowfoot might well have baulked against cold-blooded revenge, but he was not averse to

116

bending the rules to obtain vital information from a known killer. He shrugged, then stood up and walked off into the surrounding gloom of the forest. 'He's all your'n, Trace,' he remarked nonchalantly. 'Just try to avoid letting anything show when the judge questions him.'

The two old partners had practised this subterfuge before when they were members of a vigilante gang after the War. It had always worked a treat – the good guy (Cal) versus the bad (Trace). Cal sat down on a rock listening to the bleating outlaw imagining how Trace was wafting the red hot blade in his face, a sickly grin of macabre pleasure indicating his yearning to cause his victim mind-boggling agonies. In every case the threat alone had been enough to obtain the information required.

A blood-curdling scream told him that on this occasion, the victim had called Trace's bluff. But when he returned to the camp, there were no bags of gold lying on the ground. Cal maintained a deadpan expression as he chided his associate with a deliberately jovial admonition. 'Took you longer than I expected, Trace. That sensitive touch you've always brought to these sort of proceedings ain't rusty, I hope. So where's the gold?' the lawman enquired.

The jehu huffed some before responding. 'The rat claims it fell out of his shirt when he hit the water. I don't believe a word of it.'

'It's true,' bleated Rizzo, holding a hand to his seared neck. 'There's nothing left, I swear.'

'I reckoned he was bluffing. This fella don't know

117

me like you do, pard. So I let old Jim Bowie here have his say. Show him, punk,' he snarled. With some reluctance, his nervous gaze fixed on the waving blade, Rizzo lifted his hand to reveal a raw wound. 'Nobody could take that sort of punishment and hold out on me. So I reckon he must be telling the truth.'

The cynical leer faded from Trace's visage as he added, 'Though I'd still prefer to string the rat up and leave him for buzzard bait.' He shrugged, acknowledging the pledge he had made. 'But a promise made is a promise kept. We'll just have to hope that a weak-kneed judge don't take pity on him. That would be mighty irksome.'

'Well, at least we've caught the skunk, even if'n the loot has gone back to nature,' Cal observed, pouring himself a mug of coffee. 'Old Metzler will moan about it. But that's his problem, not ours.'

Trace remained taciturn. His thoughts were far removed from the loss of the yellow peril. Instead he was focusing on the forthcoming burial of his one true love, not to mention a much-admired old driver he had called a good friend. His fists clenched, the nails biting into the palms of his hand. Blood dribbled from between his fingers. Yet he felt nothing. Only an insatiable, burning desire for justice. If this guy wriggled out from under a guilty verdict, there would be hell to pay. He took a sip of hot coffee, adding a generous slug of whiskey to spice it up.

Tied to a tree that night, Rizzo was left to ponder on his fate, having been given no more than the scraps from their meal. Trace was all for letting him starve. But the lawman wanted their prisoner in reasonable shape to face a judge and jury. Talk across the smoky fire was desultory. Both men were still hesitant about how their previous friendship stood following the unsettling confrontation between them regarding the fate of the prisoner. As a result, they were more than ready to call it a day. Distant sounds of the night – owls hooting, a coyote calling to its mate, the rustle of some moving creature, the comforting crackle of the fire – helped lull them to sleep.

It was a long and protracted journey back to Tucson. An early start was called for if they were to make it within three days. On the way back, they called on Beavertail Hokum. The trapper was happy to provide them with some food and a bed of straw in the barn for the night. Once again Rizzo was tethered to a tree outside. Unfortunately for him a flash rain storm provided great amusement for his captors the next morning. Wildeblood in particular was elated. He hooted with glee. It was the first sign of anything more than pure despair following his loss. 'This cock-eyed buzzard sure is getting used to a good drenching – first the Bowl, and now this.'

The elation soon passed when Rizzo snarled out an empty threat of retaliation should he get the chance. 'No jail can hold me, big shot. You'll see,' he scoffed. 'I'll be out of that hoosegow afore you've even turned the key.'

The grin disappeared from Wildeblood's face to be replaced by dark cloud as he pulled back his arm

119

ready to hammer the skunk into the ground. Only the quick reaction from Crowfoot saved the guy from receiving a vicious beating. 'That ain't gonna do no good, Trace,' he shouted, dragging the incensed jehu away. 'We need the law on our side when he comes to trial. Beating the rat senseless ain't gonna help.'

With some reluctance Trace allowed himself to be led away. But from that moment on, and all the way back to Tucson, the lawman had to be on his guard to ensure the protection of his prisoner. Consequently he breathed a sigh of relief when the town hoved into view.

ELEVEN

UGLY RECEPTION

No sooner had the three-man contingent entered the main street of Tucson when a crowd began to gather. Cal could see straightaway that it was not a welcoming committee. The prevalence of grim faces was enough for the lawman to stiffen in the saddle. Sweat was pouring down the fearful outlaw's face. He knew exactly what these critters had in mind. And it sure wasn't a cool glass of beer to slake his thirst.

Only Trace Wildeblood appeared indifferent, blasé even, to the potential danger as the riders drew up outside the marshal's office. They dismounted to find Tiny Brazos leading a hostile pack out of the Fortunado saloon and across the street. 'Glad to see you've caught that murdering swine, Marshal,' he rasped, still clad in his white bartender's apron. 'Miss Dexter was well liked around here.'

'And don't be forgetting old Wilko Verde,' called

out a voice from the rear. 'That guy has been living here since before most of us were born.'

A murmuring of agreement saw blacksmith Seth Torrance stepping forward. 'Them murdering skunks have taken away my best pal and chess partner. Old Wilko didn't deserve that kind of retirement.' His gruff voice had taken on a grizzly rasp as a rough hemp rope emerged from behind his back. 'Ain't no need to wait on some soft judge giving these killers a light sentence. I say we string 'em up here and now!'

A growl rippled through the crowd, which was suddenly turning into a lynch mob. Cal knew he had to act fast if the law was to be upheld. 'There'll be no lynch law in Tucson while I'm marshal,' he rapped out, squaring off to face the shifting throng.

'You're only one man,' the bartender hawked out. 'Figure you can keep these rats safe on you're ownsome?' He moved forwards with the intention of grabbing the prisoner from off his horse.

'That's where you're all wrong,' a youthful voice shouted above the hostile babble. 'Marshal Crowfoot appointed me as deputy, and I'm backing his play.' Jeff Hayden had drawn his revolver and was panning it across the gathering. 'This man will face a trial with a proper judge and jury passing judgement, not some vengeance-crazed mob. Any man who figures otherwise will answer to Judge Remington here.'

The kid's vehement rebuke of the lawless threats was supported by a belligerent look challenging anybody to break the face-off. He silently prayed it would not come to pass. Inside his guts were churning with fear. Was it really him who had threatened these hard-faced men with violent retribution? It barely seemed credible. The startled wary expressions were enough to convey that the bulk of those present had likewise been caught on the hop. Nobody had expected the young deputy to be so ardent in carrying out his duties.

Cal immediately took advantage of the lull created by his deputy. 'You heard my partner,' he snapped. 'The judge will be here day after tomorrow. I guarantee it. Now all of you get about your business before somebody gets hurt.'

Jute Hubbell, the assay agent, shook his head, interjecting with a cynical rebuke of the marshal's claim: 'Last I heard Judge Bannock was heading for Globe to settle a land dispute once he'd finish his case load in Casa Grande. He ain't due in Tucson for another two weeks. What you gotta say to that?'

All eyes focused on the marshal. Cal squared his shoulders, not batting an eyelid. 'I said he would be here on Thursday, and I meant it. That is unless you have knowledge that an officer of the law ain't privy to, Jute?' The blunt contention was enough to see the agent sinking back into the crowd.

Only Tiny Brazos showed any further grit by posing a question to Wildeblood, who had so far refused to become involved in the ugly confrontation. 'You gonna let this turkey off the hook, Trace? We all know you were going to pop the question to Miss Dexter perty soon. If'n it were me I'd want justice here and now.'

The highly respected jehu aimed a sour look at the speaker. He had no wish to be reminded of his defunct ambitions in that direction. 'It was your blabbing to that crafty weasel that got this mess started in the first place,' he growled out, pointing an accusatory finger at the barman. 'So don't be getting so high and mighty now.'

'Didn't mean no harm, Trace,' the tactless barkeep blurted out. 'I had no idea he was planning a robbery. His silky tongue got the better of me. I sure am sorry. But surely you want justice for what's happened,' he finished, trying to turn the accusation off his own shoulders.

The aggrieved party remained silent for a moment as he considered the outspoken view expressed by the barman. Everybody looked his way. Time hung heavy as lead over the antagonistic gathering. His response alone would determine the prisoners' imminent fate. Finally he merely shrugged his shoulders. In truth he knew it was his own tittle-tattle that was the real cause of their troubles. 'Forget it, Tiny,' he muttered half to himself. 'You ain't the only one who played into Rizzo's hands.'

Other issues were now occupying his woeful thoughts. Even though he still harboured a festering resentment against his old buddy for preventing the ruthless extermination at Ponderosa Butte, the fire in his belly had simmered down somewhat. As a consequence he was not prepared to sanction a lynching.

'If'n this is how Cal wants to handle things, then so be it.' He turned away, shuffling across the street to the saloon. With the leading proponent having backed down from the confrontation, the others slowly dispersed, muttering among themselves.

For the time being at least, peace had been upheld – although how long that would last was in the hands of fate now, not to mention an excessive consumption of whiskey over at the Fortunado. 'Get the prisoner inside, Jeff,' Cal ordered in a quieter voice, 'before this lot change their minds.'

While his deputy hustled the wounded outlaw into the jail, Cal kept a sharp eye on the retreating crowd before following him. Once inside, the door was locked and bolted. 'Is the judge really coming day after tomorrow?' Jeff asked, somewhat unconvinced by his boss's belligerent manner towards the baying mob. 'Or was Jute Hubbell telling the truth?'

'It don't matter whose telling the truth,' Cal snapped. 'That judge has to be here damn quick or, like night follows day, we'll have a lynching on our hands.' His ardent gaze fell upon the young deputy. 'You ever seen that happen, Jeff?' A nervous shake of the head found him continuing: 'Well, thank your lucky stars, 'cos it ain't perty. When vigilante law takes over, nobody is safe. Mob rule is brutal, ugly. And once it gets a hold there ain't no going back.'

'So what we gonna do?' Jeff asked lamely.

'I want you to go over to the Overland office and tell Brad Metzler to cable Casa Grande and ask them to tell the judge he's needed here. And while you're

125

out, get the doc to come over and see to the prisoner. I want him and that other turkey fresh as daisies to stand trial when that judge gets here.' As well as being the stagecoach depot, Brad Metzler had successfully petitioned for it to become the telegraph office.

The marshal unlocked the door and cautiously peered out. The street was clear. The hammering of a piano over at the saloon gave the illusion of normality. Folks just enjoying themselves over a few friendly drinks. And over all, the moon shone down, bathing the street in a scintillating glow of peace and tranquillity. Cal couldn't hold back a sardonic guffaw, the truth being far removed from the perceived fantasy. A simmering air of tension hung in the night air – a ominous notion of imminent danger you could almost cut with a knife. The stoical lawman knew he was sitting on a powder keg with the fuse slowly burning down.

'OK, you can go out now,' he said to the deputy. 'But watch out for any trouble. The least sign and you get back here pronto.'

Jeff nodded and hurried across the street to the office of his ex-employer. He burst through the door without knocking. Something he would never have dared while working on the mud wagons. 'Cal wants you to send a message to Casa Grande and get the judge to come down here now,' he said to his old boss.

Mezler eyed the young deputy carefully before complying with the blunt request that had been

126

delivered more like an order. As it had originated from the town marshal he felt obliged to comply. 'OK,' and he instructed the main telegrapher: 'Send the message and ask for an immediate response, July.' No words were spoken while July Joseph hammered out a staccato message in Morse code. Once the communiqué was winging its way down the overhead wires, a palpable tension gripped those present as they waited for the reply to come through. Only the ticking of a clock on the wall informed all those present that time was passing by.

The sharp rattle of the keys finally shattered the heavy silence. But the reply was not the one required. 'The judge ain't in Casa Grande no more,' the operator translated. 'He's moved on to Chandler before heading for Globe.'

'Then get on to him there,' Jeff blurted out. 'This is serious. We need the guy here.'

Another fifteen minutes passed before the reply came back. The increasingly rowdy noise emanating from the Fortunado was clearly evident. The occupants of the telegraph office were becoming ever more jittery. The harsh rattle of the Morse key found them stiffening with expectation. The message when it came through, however, was anything but welcoming: 'Judge Bannock says he's booked to oversee some land trespassing disputes,' the telegrapher intoned bleakly. 'He can't get to us before next week at the earliest.'

Jeff was stymied as to what to do next. While those present in the telegraph office were scratching their heads desperately trying to figure out a solution that did not end in lynch law taking over Tucson, one man was sidling out of the door, unseen by the others.

After some thought, it was Metzler who offered the solution. 'I reckon we should get Cal over here,' he suggested. 'A firm word sent by the town's appointed law officer should help sway the judge in our favour.'

Jeff had no better proposal to offer. 'I'll get him to come over here right away.' He hustled out of the Overland office and back across the street. Cal had been avidly watching and quickly opened the door to admit him. 'Any luck?' he snapped out.

The grim expression on his deputy's face told him the unwanted result. After relaying the gist of the reply, Jeff put forward the superintendent's suggestion. 'Brad reckons a blunt message from you explaining what's likely to happen if'n he don't come will persuade Judge Bannock to drop his other cases and get down here fast.'

A bleak frown ribbed the lawman's forehead as he considered the notion. He was loathe to leave his young deputy in charge with a potential riot building up. But it looked like he had no other choice. 'I'll be back as fast as I can, Jeff,' he declared, gripping the boy's shoulder firmly. 'You're in charge now. Whatever happens, keep the door locked and don't let anybody in here except me.' He fastened a forceful look on the nervous deputy.

Jeff shook off the nervous trepidation that was gripping his innards. A grave determination to do the right thing saw him briskly nodding his head. 'Nobody's gonna get in here while I'm holding the fort.'

To Jeff the firm declaration appeared to have been spoken by someone else. Cal was counting on him to hold his nerve. No matter what he felt inside, Jeff Hayden would do his duty. Suddenly and almost before he realized it, he had been left alone. The heavy canvas blind over the barred window was tentatively pulled aside as he peered out. Across the street, a few drinkers had wandered outside and were looking towards the jailhouse. Jeff wiped the sweat from his brow, knowing exactly what their muttered conversation was about.

So far the marshal's flawed contention that Judge Bannock would arrive soon appeared to have satisfied the baying mob. But what if they discovered he had been deceiving them? He shuddered as he considered the grim consequences.

TWELVE

SHOWDOWN

Meanwhile inside the Fortunado, whiskey was being consumed at a rate far quicker than normal. Conversation was all about the robbery at Ventana Rim and the brutal deaths of two highly popular citizens. Ezra Pond had joined them and was volubly expressing his angst at having lost a good friend as well as a valuable employee in Israel Glamp.

Jute Hubbell was forcefully extolling his belief that the marshal was lying. 'I'm darned certain the judge ain't due here for two weeks,' he insisted. 'The tin star is just playing for time. I say we rush the jail and drag those bastards out and give them a taste of Tucson justice.'

'Jute's right,' concurred Seth Torrance the black-smith, slinging a full shot of whiskey down his gullet. 'Why should we wait around here and allow some hotshot lawyer to get them off with a slapped wrist?'

And so the snarling and grumbling grew in volume, men stamping their feet as the menacing aura of mob violence enveloped the gathering.

Trace Wildeblood was sitting to one side nursing his own whiskey bottle, now half empty, and staring blankly at the wall. Folks were giving him a wide birth. The simmering cauldron festering inside his wounded soul was evident to the most obtuse drinker. Nobody present in the Fortunado was going to initiate any trouble without his say-so.

Thus far Trace had not joined in the restless build-up of frustration. Unlike the angry crowd surrounding him, he still maintained a smidgen of faith that his old friend would come good. And justice would be served in a law-abiding manner. His chance to set the matter right in his own blunt-edged way at Ponderosa Butte had passed.

'So what about it, Trace?' Tiny Brazos addressed him after sidling up while collecting used glasses. 'We gonna sit here all night chewing the cud while those critters rest easy over yonder? I say we stretch their necks like in the old days so everyone can go about his business in safety.'

'It'll sure send a message out that any skunk messing with Tucson folks will be sent down the Glory Road in double quick time,' concurred a one-eyed freighter called Patch Sundown. The barman's daring intervention had encouraged others to move in closer and express their views. A further ardent suggestion from the blacksmith and others saw Trace turn a cynical eye towards the speakers. 'If'n Cal says the judge will be here on time, then I'm prepared to wait.' He then turned away and poured himself another slug. 'And so will you.' As far as he was concerned the matter was closed.

That was the moment the assistant telegraph operator lurched through the doors of the saloon and pushed his way through the heaving throng to where Trace was seated. Without excusing himself the guy blurted out the grim reality of what had occurred inside the telegraph office. 'The judge ain't coming tomorrow, Trace. The marshal was lying in the hope of buying time. Bannock won't be here until next week at the earliest.'

The noisy babble faded out as a myriad eyes focused on the wronged stage driver. His whole body tensed at the realization that his old friend had deceived them all. Slowly he rose to his feet along with those seated at the nearby tables. The glass of whiskey clutched in his hand disappeared down his throat as he drew his pistol and checked the load. 'It appears like our good marshal ain't the straight guy I figured,' he hissed. 'Now we're gonna play by my rules.' He walked across to the bar and turned down the light. 'Douse those other lights as well. Anybody in here who wants justice, follow me.'

He didn't need to shoulder his way to the door. Like the parabolical parting of the waves, the crowd separated. Trace paused at the entrance to the saloon and peered across to the jailhouse. He was well aware that Cal Crowfoot would not surrender the prisoners without a fight. Even with the bitterness of Sophie's loss eating away at his soul, Trace still retained a degree of caution. He had no wish for lives to be needlessly thrown away.

All set to march across the street, Trace paused as the door of the law office door opened and the marshal emerged. Gingerly looking around he failed to spot the gathering in the saloon doorway due to Trace's ordering of the lights to be lowered. Feeling safe, the lawman hustled down the street and disappeared inside the telegraph office.

Once inside the telegraph office Cal made sure that July Joseph delivered a hard, unyielding promise as to what would happen should the judge fail to appear on Thursday. 'Tell him in no uncertain terms that if'n he don't get down here lickety-split, he'll have two lynched prisoners on his conscience, not to mention a couple of lawmen unable to hold the mob from doing their worst.'

After the starkly blunt cable had been propelled along the singing wires to Chandler, all eyes focused on the silent Morse key. The tension inside the office was heavy with grim foreboding should the reply be detrimental. Brad Metzler and the marshal couldn't look each other in the eye, both dreading a deadly outbreak of anarchy. Only the telegrapher remained immune from the dire consequences, a man just doing his job.

Across the street Hubbell whispered 'Now what do you suppose he's up to?'

Trace shrugged impatiently. 'We'll wait for him to come out, then grab him,' he ordered. 'Once

Crowfoot has been removed from the picture, we'll have no further trouble sending a loud message far and wide that no darned killers can escape justice in Pima County.' A murmur of approval greeted this candid retort. 'Spread yourselves on either side of China Lane. When he comes past, we jump him. And not a sound from anyone. Last thing we need now is to give the game away. There's still plenty folks in Tucson who won't approve of what we're doing.'

With a potentially brutal showdown imminent, the bacchanalian effects of the alcohol so recently consumed were dissolving. A nervous strain filtered through the gathering – a certain apprehension that what they were about to condone was against territorial legislation. Yet nobody had any doubts that their forthcoming action was justified and necessary. Why wait for a trial that might not produce an acceptable result? Not many years had passed since vigilante law was the normal method of settling all disputes. And its influence was still felt by the older inhabitants, who hankered after instant bar-room justice.

Trace Wildeblood had accepted the new ways, but the death of his beloved Sophie had curdled his brain. The mob had only just concealed its presence in China Lane when the marshal emerged from the telegraph office. He had not waited to hear the result of the cable. Leaving young Jeff Hayden in charge of the prisoners was tugging at his conscience. The kid had proved his worth, but this business was his responsibility. All his thoughts were praying that the blunt cable sent to Judge Bannock would produce a positive response.

Suddenly, out of the blue, a dozen men surrounded him. Before Cal knew what was happening he had been securely pinioned, with Trace Wildeblood leading the ambush.

'You've been lying to us, Cal,' the jehu snapped facing his old friend. 'Bannock ain't coming to Tucson for another two weeks.'

The realization that his subterfuge had been exposed only served to make the lawman more determined to push the case for restraint. 'Taking the law into your own hands makes you no better than those varmints you want to hang. Let the law do it for you. That's the only way to make the territory safe for everybody.'

Wildeblood's face turned a deep purple as livid rage threatened to bubble over. His right fist bunched ready to deliver a blunt reply. But he held back, instead delivering a scornful retaliation. 'This law you're so all-fired eager to protect sure hasn't made my Sophie or the other poor suckers safe, has it?'

Cal had no reply to that brutal piece of truth. The mob leader didn't wait to hear anymore mealy-mouthed excuses. 'So now we're gonna make sure that justice is carried through in my way.' The marshal struggled to free himself, but there were too many strong arms holding him down. 'Best not make a fuss, Cal. I don't want to hurt you. But I will if'n you don't simmer down.' Growls of agreement were enough to make Cal aware that his own life was now on the line.

Yet still he tried to argue against the case. 'Jeff's in the jail looking after the prisoners. You gonna shoot him down when he refuses to hand them over?'

'The kid will come round to my way of thinking,' Trace shot back. 'Jeff knows it was a bad decision he made at Ventana Rim. So he won't stand in our way of making those skunks pay the full price.' He didn't wait to hear any further pointless protestations. 'We'll make sure you're nice and safely out the way so's you don't have to witness the end play. That way your blamed conscience will be clear.'

Trace then led the angry gathering down to the livery barn. Once inside the stable, Cal was securely tied to a post and gagged to ensure he didn't alert any passing help. 'Once this business has been completed,' Trace said, calmly addressing the bound lawman, 'you'll see that we are only doing what the alleged official law ought to do anyway. We're just not prepared to wait.'

'And maybe see them rats wriggle off'n the hook,' Brazos spat out in the lawman's face. Muttered imprecations impeded by the tight gag went unheeded. The time for talking was over. These men were beyond any plea for reason, anyway. Without uttering another word, Trace led the way outside where he was met by Etta Place.

'Where you headed, gal?' he asked rather curtly. 'It ain't safe for you to be on the street just now.'

'I'm going down to the jail with Jeff's supper,' she

replied, nervously eyeing the shifting mob accompanying the famed jehu. 'What's happening here, Mr
Wildeblood? Why are all these men looking so all
fired up and angry?' She knew exactly what was happening in Tucson. The deaths of the two well-liked
citizens had spread round the town like wildfire. But
her shock that vigilante law had once again reared its
ugly head was difficult to assimilate. Surely Marshal
Crowfoot would not allow that to happen.

'That ain't nothing to concern you,' Trace replied
trying to allay her fears. 'Now get off'n the street so's
you don't get hurt.'

But Etta was no meek-minded wallflower and
stood her ground. 'It's those men being held in the
jail, isn't it? You're going to hang them without a
trial. And where's the marshal? He and Jeff wouldn't
allow this to happen.'

'Come on, Trace,' growled the butcher, still
wearing his blood-stained apron and clutching a
vicious-looking cleaver. 'Let's get this done with.'

'We don't need no trial, lady,' Tiny Brazos rasped
out. 'Those skunks are guilty as sin for the killings
they've done. Cal's quit town and Jeff will see sense
when Trace has talked to him. Then we'll see real
justice is carried out.' Ugly mutterings backed up his
assertion as the gathering moved forwards, nudging
Etta none too gently out of the way. Their blood was
up and nothing was going to stop them.

Staggering away to the far side of the street, Etta's
fearful gaze registered acute trepidation, more for
the safety of Jeff than the prisoners. She knew he was

stubborn enough to make a show of resistance when this mob demanded the prisoners be handed over. All she could do now was earnestly pray that common sense would prevail.

Inside the jailhouse Jeff had been nervously watching how the ugly events were playing out. Being in charge of the jail guarding two villains that many of the town's wilder elements were intent on stringing up without a trial was taking its toll on his nerves. This was more responsibility than he had ever had in his life before. It was unsettling to say the least. But Cal had displayed faith in him, given him his trust. And Jeff had given his word to uphold the law. As such he had every intention of standing his ground against any incursion.

He hadn't witnessed the abduction of the marshal and was more than a tad worried when he spotted the mob approaching. Where was Cal? It was obvious that their intention was to storm the jail and take the prisoners. Quickly he made sure the door bolts were locked in place before standing back clutching a rifle in his hands. The door to the cell block was open, allowing the two prisoners to hear the ugly growls of the approaching mob. Both men were sweating fear, knowing exactly what fate had in store should they succeed in breaking down the door.

'Hey, deputy!' Rizzo called out. 'That's a lynch mob out there. You can't let them hang us without a trial.'

Jeff ignored the urgent plea. All his attention was focused on the twisting door knob. Finding their entry barred, an angry fist hammered on the locked door. 'Best that you let us in, Jeff.' It was Trace's voice, measured yet insistent, and with a slur indicating he had consumed more than a little hard liquor. 'No sense in you holding on to those scumbags in there. You know they deserve what we're gonna give 'em. So come on, Jeff. Open this door else we'll have to bust it down.' Another hard slam followed to emphasize the threat.

'I can't let you do it, Trace,' a nervous voice replied. 'The marshal is counting on me to keep 'em in here until Judge Bannock arrives. Then we'll have a proper legal trial.'

'Cal was lying to you, son,' Trace replied. 'He's skedaddled and left you in the lurch. The judge ain't coming at all. That's what ain't right.'

'The marshal wouldn't do that,' Jeff gravely butted in. 'He's left me in charge and I fully intend to uphold the law.'

'The kid ain't gonna budge, Trace,' Ezra Pond snarled. 'I say we break this door down now and get it over with.'

'I've got an axe,' the burly butcher announced, pushing to the front. 'We'll soon have that door open. Just give the word, Trace.'

Angry yells of concurrence saw the driver making a final plea. 'You heard that, Jeff. We're gonna break in, so stand back or I won't be held liable for the consequences. This is your last chance to surrender.'

'I can't, Trace. I've sworn an oath to uphold the law. Don't break in. What you're doing is wrong.'

The young lawman's voice had risen a notch as anxiety and a hint of doubt threatened to engulf his resolve. 'Please don't force my hand!' he begged.

Angry calls for action overwhelmed Trace Wildeblood's effort to secure a verbal negotiation. 'Come on, boys. We want justice, don't we?' Patch Sundown growled out to a howl of snarled agreement. 'This guy ain't gonna release them killers to us, so let's just take 'em.' More howls of approval greeted this demand as Trace stepped aside. Even if he had wanted to, the mob was too fired up by cheap whiskey to heed any rational appeal.

'I warned you, kid,' was his final declaration as Jeff backed away towards the cellblock. The rifle was trembling in his hands as the axe head bit through the door panels. Chunks of wood flew inwards. Jeff was sweating buckets. 'Come on, kid,' Rizzo's panic-induced croak pleaded. 'You gotta release us. We won't escape, I swear. Then you can take us to Casa Grande for a proper trial.'

Jeff threw an uncertain look towards the agitated prisoners, unsure what to do. Yet still he hesitated. His avowed legal duty was clashing with a mixture of self-preservation and allegiance to a highly respected friend. The crash of splintering wood in the front office told him that time was fast running out. Already eager hands were reaching through the rapidly widening hole to release the bolts. Jeff's back stiffened. His hands stopped shaking. Better to go down fighting than surrender, forever after being regarded as the cowardly tin star who failed in his duty.

Then suddenly the door flew open, crashing against the wall. And there in the doorway stood Trace Wildeblood, whose menacing expression flaunted a grim portrayal of his name. Behind him, a shifting mob was pushing forwards, eager to assuage their blood lust. Trace held them back as he cast a meaningful eye on to his young protégé.

Slowly he held out his hand. 'Give me the rifle, Jeff. You ain't gonna shoot me. I'm your friend. Ain't I taught you all about handling horses?' He took a step forwards, holding out a hand for Jeff to surrender the rifle.

For what seemed like a dozen moons, the two associates held each other's gaze. Watery eyes pleaded silently for Trace Wildeblood to back down. But there was no hint of capitulation in Trace's starkly cold demeanour.

THIRTEEN

BREAK OUT

The harsh explosion that followed tore through the babble of manic demands for lynch-law justice. Orange flame poured from the Winchester's smoking barrel. A look of shocked surprise, horror even, coated the young deputy's ashen visage. Had he really shot the revered driver? Trace staggered back. An equally disbelieving look saw the mob leader clutching his chest as he crashed into those milling behind him. Men scattered, not wishing to be tainted by the brutal shedding of blood.

The angry babble immediately faded to a hush charged with uncertainty. Blood had been spilled on the mob's side. That was not meant to happen. Every man present had fully expected the kid to succumb. But fate has a habit of biting back at the most unexpected moment. Trace sank to the floor and lay still.

Jeff could only stare open-mouthed at the dead

body. The one man he had respected above all others was now dead. And it was he who had fired the fatal bullet. Nobody moved. With their revered leader downed, the harsh reality of the grim situation they had instigated now registered on all faces. These men were storekeepers, traders and clerks, not gunslingers. But somebody had to make the first move.

And that person was the astute Squint Rizzo. Sensing that a heaven-sent opportunity for escape had been granted, he immediately took advantage of the lull. An arm reached through the cell bars and encircled the neck of the stunned deputy, who had inadvertently backed away from the conflict into the cell block. The arm tightened, choking off any cry, while Rizzo grabbed for the holstered pistol. 'You get the keys from his belt and unlock this damned cell,' he rapped at his sidekick, while keeping a sharp eye on the confused rabble. Any second now they could realize what was happening and take action.

A brusque response was needed to curb any threat of retaliation. The hammer of the commandeered pistol snapped back and Rizzo triggered two shots towards the mob. He couldn't miss at that short range. One of the bullets smashed through the front window, but the second found a human target.

Ezra Pond was the unlucky recipient. 'Aaagh! I'm hit!' he gurgled, lurching back into Tiny Brazos. Suddenly total confusion enveloped the gathering as the panic-stricken horde fought to extricate itself from the confined space.

'Shift your ass, Chuck, and get this door open,'

Rizzo urged. 'This critter's gonna wriggle free soon if'n we don't get out of here.'

Moments later the door flew open. Chinstrap grabbed the fallen Winchester and jabbed the barrel into Jeff's guts. 'Play the hero, kid,' he snarled, 'and you'll be joining those two corpses out yonder.' In the flick of a gnat's wing, a hopeless situation had swung in favour of the incarcerated outlaws. The threatening long gun jabbed the deputy in the guts, making him fully aware that an unwelcome meeting with the grim reaper was imminent if he didn't heed the outlaw's warning.

'That's better,' Rizzo growled in his ear. 'You got sense, kid. Now start backing up towards the rear door. None of those turkeys will take the chance of gunning down a lawman, so you ain't got nothing to fear if'n you keep a level head and do what you're told. Now move!' Rizzo made sure to keep Jeff between himself and the frightened mob, anyone of whom might suddenly acquire some backbone and retaliate.

Only the two bleeding bodies of Trace Wildeblood and Ezra Pond remained in the jail. A gruesome testament to the short yet brutally failed attempt to resurrect vigilante law. The retreating trio backed out into the rear yard. 'You've done us a big favour, kid,' Rizzo snorted derisively. 'But now you're surplus to requirements. Adios.' And with that he slammed the butt end of the revolver across Jeff's head. The unfortunate deputy slumped to the ground, out cold. 'OK, buddy, let's eat some dust. Only when we're over the Growlers and into Mexico can we afford to rest up.'

That was the moment their luck ran out. There was only one horse tethered in the yard.

After she had been given the brush-off by Trace Wildeblood, Etta Place had morosely retreated to her room. The eating house where she worked had been closed by the owner, who had gone to join the lynch mob. In frontier towns where the official rule of law had only recently taken precedence over anarchic control run by vigilance committees, many of the older generation still hankered after the old ways. Diner boss Ryker Strode was one such adherent. Mob rule where instant justice produced results was highly addictive to those who had previously been involved in such questionable practices.

The outbreak of gunfire had instantly drawn her to the window of her room, which overlooked the main street. Men were scrambling out of the law office in wild disarray, and without any sign that they had succeeded in their endeavour to grab the prisoners. Something had clearly gone wrong. And where gunfire held sway, the likely result was injury or death. Shock registered across the sleek contours of her face. Knowing Jeff as she did, he was more than likely involved. A hand lifted to her open mouth. He could be one of those in the firing line, even now lying in a pool of blood.

Quickly she hurried downstairs and out into the side alley. Half way down the back steps, the pounding of hoofs assailed her ears. Moments later two riders mounted on a single horse dashed past, disappearing amidst the gloom of back lots. Her obvious conclusion happened to be the right one. The prisoners had somehow managed to overpower their guardian and escape. Etta's immediate concern was for Jeff. Had he been shot and wounded...or even worse? It didn't bear thinking on.

Without thought for anything else she hurried down the twisting alleys behind the main street until she reached the jailhouse yard. The milky glow of a new moon lit up a prone figure splayed out on the dirt floor of the empty yard. She recognized her beau immediately and dashed across. Blood was dribbling from a cut on his head, but thankfully he was still alive. Etta gently cradled his head in her arms. A pained groan issued from between the kid's pursed lips. 'Don't move, honey,' the girl hushed him, carefully wiping the sweat from his brow. 'Rest easy and I'll go fetch the doc to fix you up.'

Even before she stood up, running footsteps sounded inside the jail. Brad Metzler emerged from the back door, followed by his telegrapher. He hurried across, the two of them lifting the comatose body and carrying the injured man into the jailhouse.

'What happened?' asked the fretful waitress, following them inside. 'I heard all the shooting and came a-running.'

'Looks to me like Jeff wouldn't surrender the prisoners and he shot Trace Wildeblood and Ezra Pond

146

when the mob tried to take them.' Etta gasped aloud. 'We're gonna have to wait for Jeff to explain things' Metzler continued, lifting his shoulders in a bewildered shrug. 'But one thing's for sure. Those two skunks must have somehow managed to overpower him and escape. And this is how they left him. The kid's lucky to be alive.'

The Overland boss assisted by July Joseph helped Jeff to his feet. He was just coming round, still groggy but at least able to stand. 'July's gone to fetch the doc so he can look you over,' Metzler assured him.

But Jeff's main priority was for Trace Wildeblood, and he questioned 'Is he...?' He couldn't bring himself to utter the fatal word.

'Don't worry, kid,' responded the superintendent, allaying the young deputy's fears. 'He was only grazed on the side of his head. But he's losing blood fast so we need to get him down to the hospital. But he should be all right.' He threw a sullen glance towards the other body. 'A goldarned pity I can't say the same for poor Ezra.'

Etta had been following behind. On witnessing the brutal carnage wrought by the jailhouse conflict, a scream of terror was torn from her throat. She automatically grabbed for Jeff, holding him tight, her head buried in his chest. He was now sufficiently recovered to be capable of soothing her anguish. 'Don't you fret, gal,' he whispered, 'I ain't gonna rest until those skunks are brought back to face the justice they deserve. And that will be administered by a proper court of law, not by some blood-crazy mob.'

The mindless quest for retribution brought the girl round. Her body trembled in fear. 'Are they still out there, lusting after their mindless version of justice?' Etta asked.

Metzler shook his head. 'After seeing Trace shot down most of them have come to their senses and disappeared into the woodwork,' he assured her. 'I reckon they're praying none of this comes back to haunt them.'

At that moment a familiar figure appeared in the doorway. Cal Crowfoot was accompanied by King Adderley, who was looking decidedly sheepish. The normally upright house gambler at the Fortunado had been inadvertently dragged into the unruly mob's visceral hunger for vigilante justice because of his high regard for Sophie Dexter.

'This guy just set me free from the livery stable after Trace and those other critters ambushed me.' A deadpan look settled on the discomfited dealer. Cal then walked up to the young deputy and shook him warmly by the hand. 'You come good, Jeff. I'm real proud of you.' A frown of disapproval rested on the unconscious body being stretchered out of the jail. 'King has told me everything. It was Trace's manic hunger for revenge that turned his head. And now he's paid a high price. We can only hope he pulls through. The doc reckons it'll be touch and go.'

Jeff was still mortified that he had been caught napping by the quick-witted Rizzo. 'It was my fault those skunks escaped,' he castigated himself. 'I should have stood my ground and never retreated back into the cell block like that.'

'You were taken by surprise when Trace refused to back down,' the marshal said assuaging his chagrin. 'It could have happened to anybody. But we do need to get after them fellas lickety-split, seeing as how I've just learned that Judge Bannock has agreed to get here within the next two days. That ought to settle everybody down when Brad tells them. You up for joining me on this chase, deputy?'

This was the second injury Jeff Hayden had sustained due to the havoc dished out by Squint Rizzo and his gang of lawless desperadoes. No way was he going to cry off when there was a chance to finally turn the tables on the brigands. The blow on the head had left him with a throbbing skull. But that was nothing compared to squaring the account they owed him. 'That's what you're paying me for, Marshal,' he averred. 'Sure as eggs is eggs I ain't being left behind after the humiliation those rats have heaped on my shoulders. But I'd be obliged if'n you could loan me one of those new peacemakers.'

'You've gotten yourself a deal, partner,' Cal concurred unlocking the gun cabinet and handing over a new Colt .45 complete with bone handle and a box of shells. 'You look after it. Those Colts are the best handguns ever made. The bad guys would do anything to get hold of these beauties.'

Jeff stroked the weapon like it was a newborn kitten. The Remington was tossed on to the desk as he holstered his new acquisition. But Cal Crowfoot was not quite finished yet. 'And when we get out there, just remember who's in charge,' the lawman pressed, holding his deputy's arm with a stern countenance. 'And do exactly as you're told. I need somebody at my back that I can depend on, savvy?'

'Don't you worry about me, Marshal,' Jeff insisted. 'I've learned a few valuable lessons since driving that old mud wagon. The young sprout who figured he knew it all has grown up.'

Just as they were about to leave, King Adderley made his presence felt. 'I'd count it as a personal favour if'n you included me in this posse, Marshal.' The normally cocksure gambler was shuffling his feet like a kid caught robbing the candy jar. 'I feel ashamed to have been carried along by that mob and want to make amends.'

'Glad to have you join us, King,' was the unequivocal response. 'I know how things like that can easily get out of hand. And you did well up in the foothills. Only a gambler could have come up with that idea of burning Wesker out.' The light-hearted remark eased the tension, making Adderley feel a heap better. 'Go saddle up and we'll meet at that large saguaro on the south side of town.'

FOURTEEN

SQUARING THE ACCOUNT

Cal had been right in his assumption that Rizzo and his pard would head directly for the Growlers. The one advantage the pursuers had was the fact that only one horse had been available behind the jail, forcing the absconders to ride double. Rizzo had expressed his resentment by booting the comatose deputy in the stomach. Jeff knew nothing of the vicious punishment, but had certainly felt its effect when he came to.

Once clear of town, the outlaws had headed straight for the cave that Rizzo had commandeered on his previous attempt to evade the posse led by Cal Crowfoot. He knew exactly where he was headed, and reached the cave in the early hours. Had the marshal made a more thorough search of the cave

151

on that occasion, he might well have discovered the gold that Rizzo had secreted there and was now intent on collecting.

That was the first thing Rizzo did on arrival. His original intention had been to retrieve it when the pursuing posse had given up the chase. The gold was hidden under some rocks at the back of the cave. A satisfied and somewhat relieved sigh greeted the unearthing of the loot, all eleven thousand dollars' worth. His hand stroked the tender scar on his neck. He had suffered a lot to get his hands on this loot. The thought of that hot blade made him shiver. He hadn't figured the guy would go through with it. Another touch of that iron and he would surely have caved in. Luck had been with him, and here he was, rich as Croesus.

'We'll stay here the night,' he told his buddy when the moon's fragile glow was doused by a bunch of clouds. 'It's too risky continuing in the dark in this terrain.'

After building up a small fire to boil up some coffee, they sat opposite one another, both thinking of how they were going to spend all that lovely dough. Wesker poked at the embers as he sipped the hot black liquid. The allure of the precious metal glinting in the firelight hooked the outlaw's greedy peepers. A rapacious tongue slid across his lower lip like some sinuous eel. 'So when are we gonna split the loot?' he asked, assuming there would be a fifty-fifty share-out.

Rizzo smiled. More akin to a twisted leer, it lacked

any hint of warmth, the icy glower even reaching his eyes. 'That's the point, old buddy,' he whispered while discreetly drawing a small derringer from his vest pocket. The gun was easily concealed in the dim glow of the fire. 'There ain't gonna be no split.' Another smile like a sidewinder's kiss snaked across the void separating the two men.

The small gun rose as Wesker was rapidly coming to the obvious conclusion. 'Why you dirty chiseller,' he snarled. 'Think you can cut me outa this deal? That ain't gonna happen.' He threw himself to one side, snatching at his holstered revolver. It was a gesture as futile as turning water into wine.

The upper barrel of the derringer roared, spitting out its lethal charge. The slug struck Wesker in the arm, but not before the Chinstrap managed to trigger off a reply. A panic-induced shot, it zipped past Rizzo's ear but struck the lone cayuse in the head. The poor beast had wandered into the cave: wrong time, wrong place. It staggered under the impact and went down.

Seeing his one means of escape kicking feebly in its death throes was like a red rag to a bull. A howl of manic rage issued from Rizzo's open maw as he leapt to his feet, finishing off the killer with the second bullet. At such close range these tiny weapons were as deadly as a shotgun. Wesker fell back, eyes rolling up into his head as if trying to find the hole in his forehead.

'What in blue blasted blazes am I gonna do now?' the killer railed impotently. He threw the cup of coffee at the wall, stamping around the cave in frustration. It was not until the early hours that the answer came to him. Once the realization dawned that all was not lost after all, far from it, he became much more animated. His face glowed with a frenzied eagerness to be rid of this damned cave and its grizzly inhabitants.

He recalled from his previous foray into these hills that an old trapper lived close by. The one from whom he had bought a horse. His set-up was no more than an hour's walk to the west. Gathering up only the essentials for the enforced march, namely the gold and his firearms, the outlaw set off. This time he would take what he needed and be damned. And should the old soak kick up a fuss...There was no need to describe how such defiance would be met.

In effect the rough trek took longer than expected. Even though he could remember the route taken, riding and walking were two different means of making progress. Steep inclines and stone-choked gullies now became major obstacles, especially to a man in riding boots. After four hours the tired outlaw was able to heave a grateful sigh of relief when the trapper's cabin hoved into view. He stopped, enjoying the rest, but knowing he had to keep going. That tin star and his deputy would have raised a posse and be on his tail by now.

Nevertheless he waited for ten minutes, carefully studying the cabin and its environs for any sign of movement. Rizzo was hoping that the trapper would be absent from his holding. He harboured no qualms about killing the guy, but it would make life easier if he wasn't there. Then he could collect anything he needed for the long ride over the Dragon's Teeth to Papago Pass. At least there were a couple of horses grazing in the corral.

Another five minutes indicated that the place was indeed unoccupied. So he made his way down through a stand of pine trees, pausing beside the corral to ascertain that he was alone. With no visible movement, he unhooked the gate and stepped inside the corral inspecting each horse.

The first was a skittish paint mare, clearly not yet fully broke in. When he tried slipping a bridle over its head, the animal whinnied shaking its head rebelliously. 'You sure don't pass old Squint's test of reliability,' the outlaw hawked out, moving on to the other horse, a bay that was much more compliant. 'Guess you're gonna be my ticket out of here, buster,' he breezed, leading the animal out of the corral ready to saddle him up.

That was the moment Rizzo received an unwelcome surprise. 'What in tarnation are you doing, mister?' Beavertail Hokum had been round back of the cabin clearing a blocked chimney flue when he heard the spirited mutiny from the recalcitrant paint. The only reason for such a commotion had to be some outside interference. His immediate concern was that a grizzly bear had infiltrated the corral. He was on his way round to collect the Hawken to despatch it when he was shocked to see an intruder trying to steal the bay. 'Reckon you must have a good explanation for taking a horse without asking,' he rasped.

As soon as Rizzo swung round, the trapper eyeballed the rogue desperado he had reported to the Tucson lawman. Straightaway Hokum knew he had done the wrong thing. He was unarmed and at this guy's mercy. And the ugly leer on Rizzo's face indicated there was little chance of that. Still, he tried brazening it out. 'You're the fella who bought a horse off'n me the last time we met. Why not pay up now, and we'll call it quits?'

'I ain't gotten time for no parleying,' the outlaw snapped, drawing his revolver. 'There's a posse on my tail and I need to be out of here pronto. You should have kept quiet. It would have been a whole lot safer. Can't have you scooting off and telling that posse where I am, can I?' He raised the gun, racking back the hammer to full cock. His finger tightened on the trigger. 'So long sucker.'

Beavertail knew he was staring death in the face. That was the moment a streak of grey shot out from the barn door and hurled itself at the man threatening his master. Mesquite's teeth grabbed the gun hand just as the weapon exploded, sending a bullet harmlessly into the air. Both dog and man crashed to the floor. But it was the dog who was now in control.

Bared fangs dripping saliva were all set to rip the assailant's throat to shreds when the command 'Guard, Mesquite!' rang out. Instantly the dog drew back. But its front legs still pinned the terrified outlaw to the ground, just waiting on the command to finish off his master's enemy. Beavertail quickly relieved the intruder of his armoury. 'This sure ain't your lucky day, mister,' he drawled. 'One move and that old wolfhound will rip you apart. Just remember that while I go finish the job I was doing when you foolishly interrupted me. I'm reckoning a posse will be coming after you. So we'll just wait here on their arrival.'

The mesmeric gaze of the faithful hound was accompanied by meaningful growls as saliva dribbled across the unfortunate Rizzo's ugly kisser. And there was nothing he could do about it. A slight movement of his right arm elicited a sharp nip from the dog. Rizzo cried out, much to the delight of old Beavertail. 'Didn't I tell you not to move a muscle?' he chuckled. 'That fella ain't had his breakfast yet. And you sure look a tasty treat in his eyes.' More delighted guffawing followed as the trapper disappeared to finish unblocking the flue.

Another hour passed before he deigned to give his captive some leeway. 'Back, Mesquite,' he ordered the dog, which dutifully removed itself from the captive's torso. 'You can get up now, mister,' he said, pointing the outlaw's own gun at his stomach. 'But just remember, Mesquite here is my guardian angel.' He tossed over a couple of sticks of jerky and a water bottle. 'Your breakfast. Enjoy it while you can.'

It was afternoon before a plume of dust down the valley informed the trapper that more visitors were approaching. Rizzo had been tied securely to one of the corral fence posts with Mesquite quietly sitting close by keeping watch. And sure enough it was Cal Crowfoot and his two deputies who rode into the yard ten minutes later. The three men were startled to see their quarry all ready for collection.

Rizzo was looking somewhat relieved to see them. Anything was better than having this darned mutt eyeing him up for its next meal. At least in a court of law he might stand a chance. 'This guy made the mistake of trying to steal a horse,' the trapper informed them. 'When I objected, Mesquite here took umbrage.'

Cal gave the prisoner a look of pity, knowing exactly what the dog was capable of. 'Reckon there'll be a handsome reward coming your way for capturing this galoot, Mister Hokum,' Cal announced with a grin. 'Squint Rizzo is one bad boy. And I intend to see that he pays the full price as prescribed by territorial law – once he's found guilty, of course.'

'You sure have saved us a difficult chase,' King Adderley remarked to the dog, whose tail responded with a pleased wag.

'Reckon he deserves his own reward,' Jeff added. 'And if'n he don't like steak, maybe he'd appreciate a luxury kennel with all the trimmings.'

Only Rizzo remained taciturn as his captors chuckled, along with Mesquite who appeared positively animated by Jeff's suggestion. 'Reckon you've hit the nail on the head there, deputy,' Hokum concurred. 'Hear that, boy? You're gonna have yourself a real palace to live in.' Leaving the outlaw to brood on his dodgy future, watched over by the contented wolfhound, the three other humans retired to the cabin for a few snorts of Beavertail's power-packed elixir.

The next day found the posse of three, together with their lone prisoner, wandering down the main street of Tucson. The normal babble of conversation faded as all eyes fastened on to the guy who days before had caused many of them to lose their typically stoical control. Brad Metzler was the one to break the impasse as he hustled out of the Overland office. 'The Judge arrived earlier today,' he announced, 'and is eager to conduct proceedings as soon as possible so's he can get back to his delayed schedule.'

He then looked across to where Jeff was tying up his horse. The young deputy was keen to get over to the Jerusalem Diner and tell Etta all about his adventures. But Metzler was having none of that. 'There's a stage ready to leave town in half an hour bound for Bisbee,' he said scratching his head as if it were a major problem. 'But since Trace is laid up for a spell, I ain't got no driver. Anybody here know somebody I could call on?' His concerned gaze shifted to the young deputy.

'Reckon he's talking to you, boy,' Cal said, concealing a smile.

A liaison with Etta Place was forgotten, at least for the present. 'You mean. . . ?' His mouth dropped open, unable to form the magic words.

'That's right, Jeff,' the superintendent declared breezily. 'I'm offering you the job. After what you've done to bring these skunks to justice I reckon you've earned the right to handle a full team now. Be ready to ride in half an hour.' Without another word, he went back inside the office, leaving Jeff standing there agape.

'Here you are, Jeff. Catch this,' a well-known voice called out from his room on the first floor of the National Hotel. 'You don't want to start a new job without a whip.' He tossed the special appurtenance down, which Jeff caught one-handed.

'I'm obliged to you, Trace,' he replied, a hint of shame causing his voice to crack. 'And this time I'll make darned sure to follow the rules. There won't be no backlash ever again.'

On the dot thirty minutes later, with Brad Metzler overseeing its departure, Jeff kissed Etta goodbye and climbed up on to the seat: 'I'll be back in two days, honey. Then we can talk more about our future here in Tucson.' The whip cracked, and the Concord lurched forward, accompanied by cheers and much hand clapping. A contented smile graced the youthful contours of the driver's face. Everything had come right for him in the end.